The following biography of George Sanders appeared on the dust jacket of the original edition of this book:

GEORGE SANDERS was born in St. Petersburg, Russia, under the protecting wing of the British Embassy, and without the usual I-must-be-an-actor-or-die ambition.

After taking a fling at textile research and a puff at the tobacco business, learning five languages, how to play the piano, saxophone and guitar, and how to sing in a good baritone, he finally went on the stage purely for profit. His portrayals have run the gamut from noble hero to base villain and George has enjoyed them all. The one role he has avoided, through choice, is that of the conventional type hero.

He is a good athlete, enjoys acting, has a lively interest in boats, likes to experiment with model airplanes, to make complex tobacco mixtures, and to invent electrical gadgets. Such a varied career would be incomplete without a fling at printer's ink. CRIME ON MY HANDS is George Sanders' first book; he promises that it won't be his last.

Mollie Lee
Pryor

GEORGE SANDERS

CRIME ON MY HANDS

INTERNATIONAL POLYGONICS, LTD
NEW YORK CITY

CRIME ON MY HANDS

Copyright © 1944 by George Sanders.

Library of Congress Card Catalog No. 90-80761
ISBN 1-55882-070-1

Printed and manufactured in the United States of
America.
First IPL printing June 1990.
10 9 8 7 6 5 4 3 2 1

To Craig Rice, without whom this book would not be possible.

G. S.

Chapter One

I SQUATTED, RATHER THAN knelt, over the prostrate form. I tried to concentrate on how, and at whose hand, she had met her death. Try as I might, though, I couldn't make myself believe that the wretched girl was dead, and I simply didn't give a damn who had killed her, or why.

For one thing, the heat was getting me. I was wet with sweat and my newest shirt was a six-dollar wreck. My Shetland jacket was going to be a headache for my cleaner. And I was so tired that I squinted against the bright light.

But I had to solve the case, and the important clue was in plain sight. That is, it was in plain sight to my trained eyes. The ordinary person would have missed it. The ordinary detective would have missed it, for that matter. But I, George Sanders, would see it.

I examined the body.

Her name was Velda Manning, and she was a spy. She had been killed because she had been careless. Served her jolly well right. She wasn't very likeable, anyway. She had always been too certain of her great beauty, too proud of her legs, which she flaunted at the drop of a glance.

They were on parade, even in death. She lay on her side, with her right leg extended. The left leg was bent at the knee, and the inside of her thigh was visible to an almost embarrassing extent. It seemed to me that several yards of bare, pink flesh was exposed to distract me from the more important problem of the body as a whole.

I lifted my eyes to the wound, a red mass in her chest. Her strutting breasts were not bare, but they gave that impression. As a matter of fact, she was much more exciting as a corpse than she had been as a flaunted body.

The clue. Oh yes, the clue. Must find it. Where was the damned thing? It had to be here. Ordinary eyes might pass it by, but not mine—not mine. This keen and flashing glance should seek it out, this incisive brain weigh its significance, this objective voice reveal all. And then, maybe this splendid body could go dunk itself in its private pool.

If only that bare leg were covered. I pulled her skirt down, and went back to the search. My legs were beginning to ache, just behind the knees.

I stood up. "The clue is missing," I said.

I knelt, later, on my spread handkerchief, to examine the body. I wasn't going to get my trousers dirty just because a weak-minded girl had got herself rubbed out. I wanted to wear those trousers to Melva's party that night. Provided I ever got away from this silly case.

Her leg was bare, but I was inured by now. This time I would find the clue. Now it peeked out from under the hem of her dress, a tiny gleam of brass that other eyes would have missed. Not mine.

I picked it up. I turned it between my long, tapering fingers. I frowned. This was a hard problem. She had been stabbed. Why, then, was this cartridge here? Had she been shot, too? A thorough person, this unknown murderer. Perhaps she had been strangled also.

Yes, there were the marks on her lovely throat. I hadn't seen them before, but once my keen mind took hold of the problem, my eyes knew where to look. I touched the bruises on her throat with thoughtful fingers. Silk had been used, a silk scarf.

I looked at the cartridge again. I stood up. "This," I said furiously, "is the wrong caliber!"

When I took up my examination again, I stood in a half crouch. It was a more comfortable position than the others, and it didn't wrinkle my pants.

The leg. Hello, leg. I was beginning to know every pore of that leg, every vein in delicate tracery just under the skin. That tiny hollow, just above her dimpled knee, the gentle curve of her calf.

Now, the wound. She had been shot. She had died instantly. Next, she had been stabbed, and then strangled. These latter acts were to cover the fact of shooting, to confuse George Sanders, detective. But they did not. The murderer had left his signature, just as surely as if he had written a confession and pinned it to the bulging bosom of her dress. This cartridge, this thing of metal, was an odd size, an unusual make. Only one man would have such a gun as fired this shell.

That man was the last person you would suspect, but as his name flashed in my head, the pattern was clear. His philanthropies, his kindliness, were a cloak for his true nature: spy, traitor, murderer.

I turned the cartridge thoughtfully between my clever fingers. I looked at it as if it were a crystal ball in which I saw the face and name of death.

"Channing Wommack," I mused aloud. "He is the man."

I stood quite still for a few seconds before I nudged the recumbent form with my gleaming shoe. "You can get up now, Pat," I said. "And pull your dress down."

I turned as Charlie ran over to shake my hand. He was almost maudlin, his round face flushed with satisfaction. "George, you were terrific. You were colossal."

I shrugged my shoulders. "I'm thirsty and hot. Can't somebody turn off those damned lights?"

Charlie yelled at the roof, "Save 'em!" and an electrician threw the master switch to plunge the sound stage into welcome gloom.

"If we don't get an Oscar for this one, there ain't no justice," Charlie said. He said it after each picture he directed. Thus far both justice and the Academy Award Committee had remained blind. "You wanta see the rushes, George?"

"Frankly, no. I don't care, somehow, after all those retakes."

"I'm going to fire that prop man," Charlie said.

The prop man who had put the wrong cartridge

under Pat's dress had been married just the day before. He was a nice kid.

"Don't fire him," I said. "He's tired. Send him home to get some sleep."

Charlie leered, and I went away.

Melva was in her office, her secretary told me with a roll of pretty eyes. "That's a lovely shirt, Mr. Sanders," she added. I patted her blonde permanent and left her happy.

Melva's green eyes had a gleam as they surveyed me. "Just the type," she said. "You're a handsome beast, Georgie."

"Hello, Red."

She scowled, looking like a piqued pixie. "Don't call me Red!"

"Don't call me Georgie!"

"You look so boyish in that fancy shirt, George. Sit down and rest your big feet. I want to talk to you."

She leaned back in her swivel chair, so that the sunlight through the Venetian blind slatted her green blouse with gold.

"Why don't you take a whirl at acting?" I asked. "A screen test in that outfit, with that pattern of shadows, would get you a fat contract."

"I'd rather be your agent, dear," she said. "Besides, my nose is too snub. I'd never be able to look down it, and if I can't look down my nose the way you do, I don't want to act."

"I don't look down my nose at people."

"It's your most valuable asset, George. Tell me about *Die by Night*."

I crossed my legs and lighted a cigarette. I slid my case across her desk. "This will be a shock to you. I suggest that you light up. If there's a drink in the place, I suggest that, too."

She sat up, leaning slightly forward. Concern darkened her eyes. "What's the matter, Georgie?"

"Red!"

"I'm sorry, George. I won't do it again. Tell."

"I have played my last role as a detective."

She didn't scream and wring her hands. She just sat, calm and unruffled. "Why?" she asked.

"I'm tired of detectives. And don't wisecrack about that. Here is why. The vogue is for the light-hearted playboy with a butter-heart and iridium brain to become involved in a murder situation. Now the audience knows that I, as that amateur detective, am going to triumph in the end. There's no suspense, except of an intellectual nature. The melodramatic action seeks to cover that dramatic fault, but I know suspense is lacking. I can't be whole-hearted about it when I know that I will win, no matter what."

"And so?" she prompted.

"And so the character I portray becomes a rather stereotyped person who is slightly bored with it all. I'm not acting any more; I'm just walking through the part."

"That boredom," she pointed out, "is what got you a two hundred and fifty dollar raise in *Die by Night*."

"Two hundred and twenty-five," I corrected, "after you take your cut."

She shrugged. "You don't think I'm going to give it back to you? I got you the raise."

"And that dress. I keep you well. What will you do when I quit acting? I have enough money to go along my own merry way. But I'm your only important client. Is this streamlined furniture paid for?"

"You paid for it," she said. "But you're not going to quit acting."

"No?"

"No. You can't. It's part of you. I propose to see that you get paid for doing something you'd do anyway."

"I'm not playing detectives any more, and I'm so typed I doubt if anyone wants me to play anything else."

"I do, George," she said. "I want you to play Hilary Weston."

"Fat chance," I scoffed.

"Fat contract," she substituted. "You'll put the government back in the black with your new salary."

She was serious. My mouth didn't exactly drop open, but it felt open. I'd have given my right profile to play Hilary Weston, and here she was dropping it in my lap. I had no idea I had even been considered for the star part in *Seven Dreams*. It was a part for which any actor would give his press clippings. That gentleman pirate who took frontiers in his stride, who left behind him a peopled wilderness and tax collectors, whose philosophy contributed so much to our present civilization, whose loves were as torrid as they were numberless, and who coffined his enemies while stealing their wives and fortunes—he had the color and variety of greatness. And I, George Sanders, was to play him.

"Are you kidding?" I asked Melva.

"It's all over but the signing," she assured me. "I didn't mention it to you before because I wanted to surprise you. Did I?"

"More than if you'd stuck a knife in my throat. Baby, you're wonderful. I am going to kiss you."

"Only in front of Fred, George. You leave Monday on location. Riegleman wants to get the desert shots out of the way while we have good weather. If you want the part."

"I'll do it for nothing, if necessary."

She was horrified. "Shut your big mouth!" She took up her telephone. "Get me Riegleman," she said. Presently she repeated, "Mr. Riegleman, please. This is Melva Lonigan . . . Mr. Riegleman? . . . Fine, how are you? . . . That's good. Look, I talked to George before he left. He's taking a vacation, you know . . . Left an hour ago. He's been working hard and he needs that vacation. He wants me to thank you for the thought, and he realizes that it's a good part . . . All right, a great part."

"I'm working on an invention," I muttered.*

"Besides, he's working on an invention that should make him a fortune. So I'm afraid he'd have to have a thousand dollars a week more than you offer."

I came out of my chair to throttle her. She waved me back and listened for a moment.

"Well," she said into the phone. "He was definite. And there's no question, of course, that he's worth even more than that. But I know you've got to stay inside your budget, and it's an expensive picture. Still—

---

* *Inventions are my other hobby. G. Sanders.*

. . . That's fine, then. I can still catch him at Las Vegas and he'll fly back on the six o'clock plane . . . Yes, he'll be ready to leave Monday morning."

She hung up and grinned at me. "That's a hundred bucks more for baby each week."

"That was idiotic," I said. "He might have told you to go peddle your flesh elsewhere."

"He didn't, though. He came through. I should have asked for two thousand.

"I'll buy you a drink," I said.

"Not in public. At least, not until after the six o'clock plane comes in." She frowned. "Now why did I tell him you were leaving on a vacation? Suppose you couldn't get a seat on the plane?"

"Then tell him I crawled back on my hands and knees over broken glass. I'd do it. I'm that tired of bending over corpses and looking deductive."

I should have kept my mouth shut. If there are Fates watching us, whiplashing us at the end of their strings, I must have given my particular Fate an inspiration. For it was less than a week later that I was bending over a corpse again, in the blazing light of a malignant sun, searching for clues. But when I nudged that sprawled and bloody figure, it didn't get up.

It was dead.

Chapter Two

B Y REFERRING to the shooting script, I can recreate
the scene almost exactly. It was the sequence in
the picture where the wagon train was attacked by
white thugs in Indian costume. The wagons had filed
past the cameras as the sun rose over giant sand dunes.
I, as Hilary Weston on a cream-colored Arabian geld-
ing, had carried on my flirtation with Betsy Collins,
screen wife of huge Hank Collins, my wagon boss,
under his eyes, which narrowed with sullen speculation.

She, Carla Folsom, could wear her Mother Hubbard as if it were a black-net nightgown, and she was
adequate in the part. Frank Lane, cast as her husband,
could mutter in his beard with the best, and the morning had gone well. Riegleman was happy.

"It has life," he told me, as we sat under umbrellas
while the technical crew set up for the battle scene.

Carla gave me a dark-eyed look over the rim of her
glass of Coca-Cola. "We played that scene," she
drawled, "like boy scouts rubbing sticks together,
knowing that a flame would break out any moment."

An extra came over to our exclusive little group, a

tall, slightly stooped man of middle years. He sort of pinned Riegleman with flashing black eyes. "Mr. Riegleman," he said, "I have not yet been told why I am here."

Riegleman's gloomy blue eyes scanned him as if he were a sand flea. "See Sammy," he said, in his clipped voice. "He'll explain it." As the man hesitated, Riegleman said sharply, "Well? We're busy here."

The man went back to the lounging group of bearded men and pioneer women.

Riegleman turned his long face to me. "I want you to keep one point in mind, George. During this battle, you will not quite forget the romance which is brewing between you and Carla. Hilary Weston was that kind of a guy. Even in the most critical situation, he never forgot what he had on the fire. So you will direct Frank to his post of danger, not only because he is your best man, but also because you hope he'll get an arrow through his heart and save you the trouble of killing him later. I don't want you to forget that, even when the lead wagon is set afire." Riegleman paused, caught his breath, and said, "You understand, George."

I nodded. "Something comparable to the situation in the Bible when David sent Bathsheba's spouse into battle hoping he'd be killed."

"Now we're stealing scenes from the Bible," Curtis, the boss cameraman grunted.

"Not a bad source," Riegleman said coldly. He added, "Besides, it's in the public domain."

Sammy came over, mopping sweat from his face.

"We're ready, chief. I hope to God," Sammy said fervently, "we don't have to do retakes on this. I've lost ten pounds already this morning."

Riegleman grinned at Sammy's tubbiness. "If you lose fifty more, Sammy, I'll make a matinee idol of you."

Sammy patted his paunch. "I wouldn't play such a dirty trick on my best friend."

After a final check, we went into action. I rode back and forth before a camera, shouting orders, placing my men, forming the wagons into a circle. I gave Carla a long, calculating look, and sent Frank into the front line.

The marauders poured over a sand dune on calico ponies, and the air was scrambled with shots and shouts. They shot several hundred feet of film, with pseudo-redskins galloping idiotically around the circle of wagons, the grim pioneers potting away, with me firing my two Colts at random, but with uncanny accuracy.

Then, signal whistles broke through the din, and the battle was over. Cameras were moved, to record the retreat of the thwarted thugs, while we shot gay, blank charges into their dust cloud. I registered mild disappointment, in a close-up, that Frank was still among the living, flicked Carla another significant glance, and we knocked off for lunch.

Prop men gathered up the guns. Sammy himself took mine, as they were museum pieces. Corpses, scattered inside and out of the wagon circle, got to their feet and ambled over to the commissary. I washed my hands under a pressure tap and started for my chair, where somebody would bring me some lunch.

That was when I saw the body, sprawled realistically behind a wagon wheel, carbine beside it. Some overly conscientious extra, I thought, who supposed that he had to play dead until he was carried off on a stretcher.

"Chow!" I called to him. "Comb the sand out of your beard, fella, and come after it."

The figure didn't move, and I knew that he was dead. The body had a look of death about it. It isn't exactly describable, but my sensation was definite. I walked over for close examination.

I knelt over the body, thinking that some poor devil had suffered a heart attack. I tried to rouse him, even then not fully believing that my conviction was justified. I nudged him. He didn't move, and the reason was there in plain sight: a small, blackened hole in his right temple.

I thought of the many times I had knelt so, before cameras, and of my scripted reactions. Here was death. Analysis was necessary, and sufficient, to determine the cause of death and to map an unerring path to the killer. But I didn't react in that fashion. I felt helpless. This keen and flashing glance did not seek out the telltale token dropped in haste. There was no clue, and if there had been, this incisive brain would not have weighed its significance.

My thoughts were completely on the sad side. This man had hired out for fifteen dollars a day, so that he could pay his back rent, perhaps. It was a sad thing that he had met death here, accidentally.

It had to be accidental homicide. The carbines which had been fired with such effusion had been loaded with blank cartridges. Responsibility for this devolved finally on Sammy, but it was quite conceivable that, somehow, one of the cartridges had not been blank.

That it had found its way so exactly to a vital spot in one of the actors, rather than having been shot harmlessly over the head of balked bandits, was a long coincidence, but possible. I've collected on some of the four-legged ones.

I kept in mind, however, the possibility of murder, as I went for Riegleman. It would have been a good stage setting for murder, with the cavorting, the shooting, the hubbub of make-believe. Yes, an enemy could have drawn a bead on his victim and let him have it, with a good chance to escape later reckoning with the law.

But if that was the way it had happened, it was possible that the murderer had been photographed in the act. A battery of cameras had recorded the scene from various angles. I filed that thought away for future reference, too.

"I say," I said to Riegleman, "come for a short stroll with me. We have a corpse to contend with."

He put down his paper plate and fell into step. "I was afraid of something like this," he muttered. "Too much sun, I suppose, for some guy with a hangover."

"A bad combination," I agreed, steering him toward the fatal spot. "But it seldom shoots a man through the right temple."

Riegleman halted. "My God!" he said, in stunned tones. "You're kidding."

"I'm sorry. I wish I were."

"But it's impossible! All the guns were supposed to be loaded with blanks!"

"Apparently somebody improved on the script."

"How in the hell," he demanded, "will we ever find who fired the shot?"

"Someone in that moil of beards probably fired it," I suggested. "But I'm not sure that determining who will be necessary, provided that we can prove it was accidental."

"Prove it? Of course it was accidental. By the Gods," he went on grimly, "if I can find out who was responsible for a loaded shell getting into a gun, I'll have his hide."

"First of all," I said, "we'll have to get the local authorities out here. It's a matter for the sheriff and the coroner."

"There goes my shooting schedule," Riegleman groaned. "Well, let's have a look at the poor guy."

Riegleman scowled down in accusation at the corpse. This was a monkey wrench in the machinery. This meant delay, which in turn meant loss of money, which in turn was painful to him.

"Just a young fellow," he said. "Too damned bad."

"Do you know him?"

"Never saw him before. Maybe Sammy knows him." He took a whistle from his pocket, blew it, and beckoned to Sammy, who was carrying two plates from the commissary.

Sammy gave the plates to a man near him. His gestures indicated that the plates were to be guarded to the death, if necessary. Then he approached us unhappily, sinking deep into the sand at each step. He said, "George, about your pistols—", but fell quiet as the director waved a hand.

Riegleman indicated the body. "Do you know him?"

"Oh, God!" Sammy moaned. "He's dead!"

"Don't go psychic on us," Riegleman snapped. "Who is he?"

"I don't know. Maybe Paul will."

"Get him!"

Sammy turned a white, round face upward at Riegleman. "Please, chief. I don't feel so good. I've got to sit down somewhere."

"I'll go," I said. "Who is Paul?"

"He's the casting director."

Paul looked as if he had just run three blocks to catch a Brooklyn bus in July. "My God," he said. "What does that slave driver want now? I'm busier'n a tick at a horse show. Oh, well!" He came out of his trailer-office. "What gives?" he asked me.

"One of the extras got himself killed. We thought you might be able to identify him."

"So that's why we had one lunch left over? I thought at first Sammy maybe only took one. I've been checking the cast to see if we're paying somebody who's not here."

"Did you find anyone missing?"

"Yeah. Guy named Herman Smith. Didn't get his lunch. Showed up for work, turned in his slip okay.

So I guess he's it. What'd he do, get a horse hoof in his face?"

"He got a bullet in his head."

"Yeah? Thought they shot only blanks."

"That was my impression, too."

We walked over to Riegleman. He stood some distance away from the body. Sammy was under a wagon near him.

"Well, we know who he is," I told Riegleman.

"Yes, Mr. Riegleman," Paul said eagerly. "The chef informed me that we had an extra lunch, and I checked to see if somebody had turned in his work slip and then taken a powder. I watch that sort of thing very closely."

Riegleman nodded shortly. "Will you take a look, Paul? I have sent for the police."

Paul looked down at the bearded face. He frowned. He looked up at Riegleman, then back at the corpse. "I'll be a son of a gun," he said. "That ain't Herman. I never saw this guy before."

Chapter Three

HAVE YOU EVER seen a group of youngsters rough-housing each other? Remember how, if one falls unconscious from an accidental blow, they all stand aimlessly for a few moments staring blankly at the unlucky victim?

We did just that. We looked down at the nameless corpse as if we hadn't seen it before. With a name, it would have been one of us, and our emotions would have been personalized. Nameless, it was a stranger in our midst, and we eyed it curiously, as Kentucky mountaineers were reputed to examine a well-dressed stranger. Was he just a visitor, or was he a revenuer?

Riegleman showed resentment rather than any other emotion. His razor-thin mouth was a tight, angry line, and his hard blue eyes seemed to send out sparks of indignation. This was understandable, knowing Riegleman. A corpse—worst of all, a nameless corpse—was threatening his already tight shooting schedule.

Paul pushed a thin white hand through black hair and frowned at the unknown. His thoughts were fairly obvious. A "ringer" had slipped in on him, and

Riegleman would want to know how it had been done. Paul's thoughts were concerned with his job.

Sammy just gaped. If Sammy had thoughts at the moment, they slumbered.

I tried to analyze my own feelings. When Paul had said that one Herman Smith was missing, I had immediately begun to wonder why anyone should want to kill him. For I held to the possibility of murder. If it should prove to be accident, the matter was done. But if it were murder, there was need for thought and investigation, all necessarily based on his identity.

And here we had a stranger. A dead end for thought. You cannot find a motive for the murder of a completely anonymous person. You must know his habits, associates, and enough of his background to determine why his death was desirable to one or more persons. It would be possible for a murderer to kill with impunity as long as the corpse remained anonymous.

I became aware that Riegleman, Paul, and Sammy were looking at me. I gave them what has come to be known as my quizzical expression and said nothing, loudly.

"This is in your field, George, old boy," Riegleman said.

I tapped a cigarette against my thumbnail, looked as disinterested as I could under the circumstances, and said, "Oh?"

"It's a mystery," Paul said. "That's your dish."

I didn't like the way he said it. He was too eager to place a burden on me, too eager to overlook his particular responsibility.

"I was under the impression," I said casually, "that the casting director was expected to be familiar with the extras."

Paul flushed as Riegleman's gaze swung to him. "It's the beards," he said apologetically to Riegleman. "You can't expect anybody to tell 'em apart. This guy's supposed to be Herman Smith, according to my records. Everybody else was checked off at lunch. If he's somebody else, can I help it?"

Riegleman didn't answer, and Paul flushed again. He flashed me a venomous glance and turned away.

Sammy made his single contribution to the investigation. "Hey," he called from under his wagon refuge, "how about a social security card?"

"Of course," Riegleman snapped, and knelt by the body.

"Uh-uh," I said. "Mustn't touch. Clues, you know."

Not that there were any clues. At least, I couldn't see any. How different this was from my screen plays. As *The Saint,* or *The Falcon,* I had been confronted many times with situations more baffling than this, and always I had penetrated brilliantly to the heart of the matter, seen a clue, reconstructed the situation and acted unerringly. But here was a nameless bearded corpse sprawled inside the circle of wagons on baking sand. There were no dropped collar buttons, no cartridges of an odd caliber, no telltale footprint with a worn heel, no glove lost in haste.

It seemed as if somebody had simply thrown away an old corpse he no longer needed.

I began to wish that we could throw it away too. If there was one object that we didn't need, it was a corpse. Especially one with a beard, with no name, and with a spurious work slip.

I could almost hear wheels of thought spinning in Riegleman's long skull as he glared down at the body. *Seven Dreams* was on a tight budget. He had planned to shoot these outdoor scenes in two or three days. An investigation into the death of this man would throw the shooting schedule off.

An investigation was under way even at that moment. The rest of the company, with an almost clairvoyant curiosity, was moving toward us in a close-packed, muttering group. I walked to meet them.

"Don't come any closer!"

They stopped. I told them that a man was dead, and that they should stay away until called. "One of you may be able to identify him, but the police should look over the scene before we track it up. Please go back and make yourselves comfortable."

They did, and I returned to Riegleman's side. "I hope you don't mind my taking charge that way," I said.

He shrugged. "Sammy!" he snapped.

Sammy gave him a sidewise look from under the wagon.

"Sammy, you had charge of the ammunition in those carbines. Every cartridge was supposed to be blank. What have you to say?"

"What can I say?" Sammy replied. "Evidently at least one wasn't blank. Is that my fault? Am I supposed to examine thousands of cartridges, one at a time?"

Riegleman seemed to drop that line of thought. "It

seems strange," he muttered, "that the shot should have gone so exactly to a vital spot. There's an almost geometrical precision in that wound. Dead in the center of his temple."

"It's just a freak accident," Paul said. "Like cyclones."

Riegleman gave him a puzzled frown. "Cyclones?"

"Sure," Paul went on. "I remember one that blew a farmhouse all to hell and gone, but picked up a basket of eggs and set it down a mile away without breaking an egg."

"What *are* you talking about?" Riegleman demanded.

"I'm simply saying that the impossible can and does happen all the time," Paul said. "If one shell was loaded in all those carbines, it's not hard to believe that it smacked this poor guy dead center. It's no harder to believe than that egg story."

Riegleman thought this over. "Yes," he said finally. "I believe it is better that way. The accident theory will let us stay on schedule. Shall we agree on that?"

He gave the three of us a questioning glance. Sammy's fat face became flaccid with relief; an accident story would relieve him of responsibility. Paul's dark, thoughtful face indicated furious thought. He was examining the idea from all angles.

I said, "The mysterious stranger."

Riegleman frowned. "So?"

"Suppose," I amplified, "that we accept the possibility of somebody getting smack in the way of a slug. It strains credibility, but suppose we accept it. Then I submit that we cannot accept that the person shot should be the only one in three hundred persons who is unknown."

"You're making it murder!" Paul exclaimed.

"I'm not making it anything. I'm analyzing. Someone else has already made it murder—maybe. We have to consider it."

They considered it. They didn't like it. But whatever they were going to say about it was cut off by a low moan that drifted nearer across the sand dunes. A siren heralded the approach of lawful authority.

This was Gerald Callahan, sheriff, and his deputy, Lamar James. The big sedan which carried them swirled up to us in a cloud of dust, a rear door popped open and a man rolled out like a barrel of beer.

He was squat and round, with a froth of white hair and ears like the handles of a beer mug. He hung a smile between his ears and came over to us. I tensed my shoulders against a slap on the back. A good thing, too; I think he tried to knock me down.

"Name's Callahan," he said, with a bull-like friendliness. "Call me Jerry. Sheriff in these parts. Now, what's the trouble?"

I introduced myself and the others, and waited for somebody else to tell him.

Riegleman said, "We seem to have had an accident here, and since it was fatal, we thought you should know. I had you notified. Here it is."

Callahan looked at the corpse. "Shot, hey?" This piece of intuition brought a small silence. Callahan frowned in a helpless sort of fashion, then yelled at his deputy. "Lamar! Come here, will you?"

The deputy came out of the car like brown paint

from a tube. He was slim, tall, and dark. He lounged over to us, was introduced, and took a look. He said nothing. He waited.

"Who's going to tell it?" Callahan said pleasantly.

Riegleman told it. He pictured the scene that was to look like the real thing on the screen and, we hoped, bring from the critics such phrases as "realistic drama," "a thriller," and so on. Riegleman turned the story conference over to me, and I related how I had found the body.

Then we all stood silently for a moment.

Callahan broke the silence. "Looks open and shut. The guy got in the way of a slug. One of the shells wasn't blank. Hey, Lamar?"

The deputy's long, brown face showed no expression. His tight mouth cracked. "Caliber?" he asked. "What size shells in the carbines?"

We looked at Sammy. "Forty-fives," he said.

James knelt beside the corpse and looked at the blackened hole in the temple. He looked for a long time. When he raised up, he was frowning. "Thirty-eight," he said.

He sounded like me, in one of those *Falcon* roles. He didn't have the polished manner, of course; he wasn't supposed to be a light-hearted Briton. But he tossed in the surprise twist with the same casual aplomb.

"I don't see how you can tell," I objected, "just with a quick glance. There are too many factors. You can't see the slug."

The sheriff bristled. "If Lamar says it was a thirty-eight, it was a thirty-eight. He don't make mistakes."

I shrugged. "It could be. I'm no expert in these matters. But I still don't see how he can tell."

"Does it matter?" Riegleman asked.

Callahan looked bewildered. "I don't know. Does it, Lamar?"

James said thoughtfully, "If all the carbines were forty-fives, somebody shot him with some other kind of a gun. Anybody carry thirty-eights?"

We all looked at Sammy again. He shook his fat face from side to side. "Nobody," he said.

My mouth had a tendency to drop open, which I fought with clenched teeth. Sammy knew that somebody had carried .38's. I had. The two Colt revolvers, with silver-inlaid handles, with which I had popped away, were .38 caliber Colts, on .45 frames.

And Sammy knew it, too. He beetled his brows at me in an expression of warning.

I said nothing.

Chapter Four

LAMAR JAMES NARROWED his dark eyes. After a moment he said, "Better look at the guns. Where?"

Sammy waved at a cluster of trucks. "There."

James looked at the corpse. "Blanket."

"I'll get one," I said. I went to one of the wagons and started to pull out a Navajo pattern.

Underneath it was a gun.

The gun had a silver-inlaid handle and it was a .38 Colt on a .45 frame. It was one of the pair Sammy had issued to me.

And I fell right into an old familiar role. I did it automatically, without thinking. Once again I was the gifted amateur loggerheading the clumsy cops. With a graceful gesture which was to appear part of the one I'd already started, I let the Navajo blanket fall back over the gun and picked up another, darker blanket. As I carried it out of the wagon I took out my slim silver case and casually lighted a cigarette to think on.

Here I was again, back in the pattern. A nameless corpse, and the only clue to the killer was my gun, planted by a nameless hopeful who thought he could match wits with me. Only, this time the lines weren't written for me. I had to make them up as I went along.

I gave the blanket to James and he placed it over the corpse, asked Paul to remain on guard, and led the way across the sand toward the trucks. I fell in beside Sammy, and we lagged behind.

I didn't tell Sammy about the gun. Oh, no. That was my secret, to be sprung as a surprise at the psychological moment when the murderer was sure he was in the clear. Then the cops would look chagrined, the killer would make a break for freedom, only to be cut down with a bullet in his thigh.

Then we would have a long scene where I modestly explained why I had suspected the guilty party from the beginning, and how twitch by twitch I had drawn the strings of the net about him.

All I needed to round it out was a suspect. I had Sammy, but his actions didn't fall into any psychological pattern. So, instead of telling him what he was doing, telling him in a detailed deduction that would drop his jaw down to his knees, I said,

"Now, maybe you'll tell me what the hell is going on."

"Why did you do it, George?" he asked. "I wanted to wait to ask you before I said anything. Maybe you had a good reason. If it's good enough, I'll string along."

"Do you mean," I asked with a flash of understanding, "that you think I killed him? Why? And why did you say that everybody carried forty-fives?"

"Well, about your guns, George, sure, I know

they're thirty-eights, but something funny happened.
I gave you a matched pair, very valuable. And what
I got back was not a matched pair. One of 'em was
a modern thirty-eight police special, Smith & Wesson
side ejector. I wanted to ask you how come." He hesitated. "And where's the other gun? That pair cost
dough. Belonged to Cody, or Jesse James, or somebody like that."

"That's idiotic," I said. "The guns I used in the
scene were the guns you gave me. When the scene
was over, I shoved them back in my holsters. They
stayed there until you took them up."

"One of 'em didn't."

After all, I thought, I had only Sammy's word for
this. I decided to let him do the talking, and to stay
close to him.

"What did you do with the guns, Sammy?"

"I put 'em in a safe place. I wanted to talk to you
before I turned 'em in."

"Then somebody is going to ask what happened
to my guns."

"We can handle that. There's a pair of forty-fives
in the arsenal. We can say you carried them."

I stopped. He turned his fat face to me. "Sammy,
I don't want any part of this. You're hiding evidence,
and you're making me an accessory. I have nothing
to hide, so let's turn in the guns."

"Now, wait, George. Let me ask you something.
Suppose that odd gun was used to kill the poor egg.
Suppose you didn't do it. Somebody did, and somebody switched guns on you. You're in for trouble if
you can't find out who switched 'em."

"You're the obvious choice."

"I know that," he said earnestly, "but I didn't do it. So here's what I figured. Maybe you'd like to do some snooping before we mention this to the cops. Maybe you could find out who did it and turn him in."

His suggestion had merit. If the odd gun should prove to be the murder weapon—for it was murder beyond any doubt now—and someone stumbled on the fact that I had carried it, the police might assume that I had fired it. And my own theory, that coincidence had no place in the shooting, could be turned neatly against me. I could wind up in the state gas-chamber.

On the other hand, I knew that I hadn't fired any but the two pistols originally issued to me. And, going back over the battle scene in my mind, I knew that I hadn't even pointed a gun in the direction of the dead man.

This latter point I might be able to prove. So far as I knew, I had been under the eyes of one or more cameras during the entire scene. The rushes would show my every act. Though there was a possibility that I was out of camera range at one time or another, and I would have no alibi for that time.

This brought up the question of who had switched guns on me. When the scene had ended, a man came up to take my horse. He could have done it. Then I had joined a group of principals and executives discussing the scene.

I tried to remember who was in the group. There were Carla, Frank Lane, Wanda Waite, Riegleman, the script girl, the head cameraman, and the sound man. We had babbled and bubbled. The switch could have taken place then.

Assuming, of course, that somebody *had* switched guns on me. Sammy could have done it when he took them up. He had opportunity to ditch the extra gun in that wagon.

His gray eyes were steady on mine. "Well, what do you say, George?"

I didn't say anything for a moment. If Sammy had switched the guns—and therefore was a murderer— what could he gain by denying that I had carried a pair of .38's? It seemed to me that his best play was to admit that I had carried them, and let the law have its way. Maybe he really was trying to help me.

"All right, I'll go along with you, Sammy."

"Then we'd better get over to the truck."

The guns had been packed away in cases. It didn't take long to go through them. There were no .38's.

As I watched, I wondered why anyone should have tried to involve me in the killing. I hadn't been in the company long enough to make enemies. Of course, the major reason might not concern me personally: I was the only one in the cast with side arms. What better place to hide a murder weapon than in my holster, assuming that Lamar James was correct and the killing had been done with a .38? Yes. That was probably it.

James turned to Riegleman. "You the boss here?"

Riegleman twisted a little smile at him. "Yes, as long as Mr. Wallingford isn't around. He's the producer."

"He's not here?"

"Not yet. I expect him."

James said, "Send 'em down one at a time. Got to find out who the guy is."

Riegleman flicked a hand at Sammy. "Get at it."

Sammy gave me a mournful look and waddled away. So we couldn't go further into this thing at present. I didn't like it, but I could do nothing but keep an eye on the wagon where the gun was hidden. I took a chair under a beach umbrella and watched.

Peggy Whittier, the colorless little script girl, smiled at me brightly from a nearby chair where she worked on her notebook. Corpses couldn't disturb her; she had an exacting job recording all pertinent details of the scene. If it should need to be shot over, she would know how it should look.

I was more worried than I cared to admit to myself. I had been faced with worse situations than this many times. As *The Saint*, or *The Falcon*, I had had circumstantial evidence point an evil and convincing finger at me. I had always escaped and turned the tables on the dastardly villains who wished to eliminate me. Only, some ingenious fellow had always written the script for me.

This actuality was disturbing. At one time or another, if I could believe Sammy, the fatal gun had been in my possession. I could just see myself convincing call-me-Jerry Callahan that I was ignorant of the fact. That sterling idea-a-year man would pop me into the clink and swallow the key.

As I watched the cast go one by one down by the wagons and look at the corpse, I made up my mind to take Sammy at his word. It was not a sensible decision, and I was aware of it at the time, but I made it. Sammy had something naïve in his make-up. Not that it justified my believing him; but it caused me to.

I was about as objective as a mother who takes a smoking gun from her favorite son and swears that he never fired it. And I didn't feel paternal toward Sammy; I felt a little sorry for him. He had been a dancer, once. He had done all right. When he danced in his hey-day, it was feathers in the breeze. Then he had begun to gain weight, his arches commenced to scream.

He had entered Hollywood through a side door as a writer. Not that he could write; but that didn't matter, then or now. He was later given an under-financed quickie to direct, but the producer fled with the funds, and Sammy knocked around for some time in thinning soles. Finally he landed with Riegleman, being a sort of office boy called assistant director.

Somewhere along the line he could easily have accepted a feud. He could have waited until today, and killed his man. Perfectly possible, but I didn't believe it; Sammy was no killer.

This reflection was secondary to my keeping an eye on the actors as they reviewed the corpse. As one returned, another went down to Callahan and James. Presently, one stayed a little longer than the others. He was a slim man in a white Stetson. He talked with the officers, James wrote in a notebook, and he came back. Sammy intercepted him.

I started for him, but he drifted away, and Sammy met me.

"The body's got a name now," Sammy said. "Severance Flynne."

The name meant nothing to me. I said, "Excuse me, Sammy, I want to see that fellow who identified him."

"He can't help you, George. He never saw the guy before."

"How," I asked, "did he identify him, then?"

Sammy grinned up at me. "He was doing Wanda Waite a favor. She didn't want to make the identification, so she asked this lad. She told him who the dead guy was, and no more."

"Let's go see Wanda, then," I said grimly.

"Aw, George," Sammy objected. "It's kind of obvious why Wanda wouldn't want to identify him. He was a good-looking cuss." He paused. "You know Wanda."

"All I know is she's a hard-working actress and a nice person to have around."

"Well, she made her name as the missionary's wife in *China Will Wait*. She's been playing parts like that ever since; the earnest, honest, kindly, courageous girl."

"And so?"

Sammy frowned. "You can see what it would do to her screen career if her public knew she'd identified a murder victim. Think of the inferences. Hollywood's just full of artists who draw nothing but inferences."

"If she knew Flynne," I said, "she might know who'd want to murder him. Maybe she'd like to have us drop in for tea."

Sammy looked at me gloomily and finally said a reluctant "All right."

Wanda was in her trailer dressing room. When she let us in, I had the impression that she had been sitting before her mirror, just looking. I didn't blame her.

The effect was disturbing. Because suddenly she seemed like someone else. To me, Wanda had been a good actress and a good kid, not caring who saw her with her hair in curling pins, and trading cracks with the best of them. But this Wanda was a composite of all the sirens from Lilith to Theda Bara.

Beautiful, too, with her satin-blonde hair and her scarlet mouth. She could have raised a pulse in the Rushmore memorial.

Her costume added to the effect. She still wore the Mother Hubbard affair, but it was tailored, and she put a strain on the seams of her bodice.

She opened a catalog of implications with, "Can I do something for you?" She sounded like a one-woman wolf pack.

I decided to play along. I said, "I shouldn't be surprised."

"I think you would," she said huskily.

It was then I put a finger on the really disturbing factor: she was like an actor unsure of his lines who wanted terribly to make good. Her timing was just barely off; she was overacting to the faintest degree. Why? What was eating this girl who was a saint in the eye of a camera? I filed the question for future reference.

I said, "Tell me about Severance Flynne."

Her eyes cooled a little, became a little more like blue marbles than star sapphires. She said nothing for a few moments. Then, "I don't know anything about him."

"But you knew him?"

"Barely," she said. "Met him on the train yesterday. We talked."

"What about?"

"Him. What else? He came out here from Nebraska. He played enough extra roles to keep him not more than a month behind in his rent. He got into this rat race because of a hangover. Herman Smith was hired, but he went on a bender the night before he was to leave. He woke up with a skull full of rivet guns, and asked Severance to take his place. Severance had a beard, and that was all that was necessary. So—"

"Somebody killed him," I said.

"What would you want me to do?" she asked. "Rush down and say I knew him? I'm trying to build up a reputation as an actress. I've got to keep my skirts clean." She added, "In public."

I ignored the distracting invitation. I said, "I see. Did he mention knowing anyone in this company?"

"He said he didn't know anybody. He knew you, of course, by reputation. Who doesn't?"

I got to my feet. "Thanks for the help."

"It's nothing, sir," she said. "Come back—any time."

She almost out-leered me—I, who had made a fortune pushing leers at lassies and lenses—but as I
turned away I caught a brief shadow in her eyes.
She was worried. I filed away that fact, too. My
mental cabinet was getting quite cluttered up. Nothing seemed to fit into the proper cubby holes. A little
spring cleaning seemed indicated.

Out in that furious sun once more, I said to
Sammy, "I don't like to play this way. Let's turn in
the guns and tell the sheriff the truth. After all, I
have nothing to fear, and the information may help
that deputy. He seems shrewd."

"I guess maybe you're right, George. I hope you
don't get caught in the middle. Come on. They're
in my office."

As we wound through the trucks, a messenger
caught up with us. He flashed white teeth out of a
nest of freckles. "The cops want to see you guys,"
he said. "They found the gun hidden in a wagon."

"We'll be right along," I said. He went away, and
I looked at Sammy. "We're a little late, but all we
have to do is tell the truth."

"I hope so," Sammy muttered. "Here we are."

We went into his trailer office. "Now if this plot
were running true to form," I said, "the guns would
be gone."

Sammy opened a drawer. He peered into it. He
opened another. Very slowly, he turned to me. His
eyes had a chill in them. His voice was steady and
thoughtful.

"It seems damned funny, George, that you'd know
it."

Chapter Five

HERE IT WAS AGAIN. Circumstances conspiring against the beleaguered hero. I can see now that I was not consciously playing the role of protagonist, but I had been cast in so many such epics that I dropped naturally into the part.

"I'm omniscient, Sammy," I said. "Here is something else that I know. We are up against someone who is shrewd and brilliant. He has courage. When something goes wrong, he improvises a solution. And something *has* gone wrong; thereby we may hang him by the tail."

Sammy remained cold. "Don't be so flip. What are you talking about?"

"Let us look at the murderer's plan, Sammy. Let us probe it with analytical eyes. First, he wishes to kill someone, and he does not wish to die for it. So he selects me as the goat. He gets his man, plants the gun on me. But it isn't found on me. That isn't in the schedule. Now, he could see you take the gun, and he could follow you here. He then steps inside and takes the gun away."

"But why?" Sammy objected. "If I'd done it, I'd want nothing to do with that gun again."

"That is because you are only a conventional murderer, Sammy—potentially, that is. You follow the pattern: conk the victim, ditch the gat. But our murderer has some obscure and, you may be sure, sensational move in mind. Perhaps he has selected another goat. We have him on the run, Sammy. He has come out of anonymity. He has a name now."

"Do you know who it is already?" Sammy asked, with a touch of awe.

"Not definitely," I said. "I mean that we know something about him that we didn't know before. Up to know, we knew only that he wanted to kill a man. He figured out beforehand how to go about it with a minimum of risk. He took the means and opportunity, then got rid of the evidence. But now we know that he has initiative. He will take chances when necessary. So that narrows our search. We can eliminate you and me, for example, from the list of suspects. I'm horribly lazy, and wouldn't have done anything about an unexpected development beyond rearranging my story to fit the circumstances; and you'd have been afraid to depart from the plan painstakingly thought out."

Sammy's eyes became steely again. "If I'd shot the guy, would I have said anything to you about the gun? How did I ever get on that list?"

"I don't mean that, Sammy. I mean that you are excluded on psychological grounds, as I am. We are now looking for someone who is capable of the action I have just described, who has initiative and courage."

Sammy said, "Yeah. Meantime, the cops want us!"

"I had forgotten. We'd better toddle along. My experience in the drama is that unless you are guilty you should never keep the police waiting. When you are, of course, you keep them waiting until the final curtain."

They were shooting questions at a white-faced Carla when we arrived at the scene of the crime. I wondered why, then realized that my gun had been in her wagon, only a few feet from the corpse.

The gun itself was between Lamar James's feet, tied inside an open paper box with a couple of loops of string, so that it could be transported without disturbing fingerprints. My fingerprints. They must be all over the gun. And our story was that I had carried .45's. I would deal with that when I was asked.

"If you didn't know the deceased," Sheriff Callahan said doggedly, "how come you shot him?"

"But I tell you I didn't shoot him!" Carla said hysterically.

"It sure looks open and shut to me," Callahan went on. "It'd be an easy shot, even for a woman, at that distance. And nobody was in that wagon with you."

"Are you disputing the lady's word?" I asked.

Sheriff Callahan whirled on me. Not whirled, exactly, it took some time to get his bulk into motion. Rather, he revolved.

"Yep," he said.

"Then you're no gentleman. She didn't shoot him."

"How do you know?" Callahan snapped.

That raised a question, all right. How *did* I know? I saw the answer clear, suddenly, and hoped that Sammy would follow my lead. I looked over the group before answering. All were looking at me: Paul, Sammy, Carla, Lamar James, Riegleman, the mousy script girl, the head cameraman, and a few others. McGuire, chief of the properties department, was not present, which was well.

"In the first place," I said, "that is not the murder weapon. In the second place, it was loaded only with blanks. In the third place, she wouldn't shoot a man in cold blood."

I had the spotlight now, and I faced them easily, a smile toying with my mouth. I made a ritual of lighting a cigarette. Lamar James, who had been quietly watching, moved forward.

Sheriff Callahan held James back for a second, asked, "You're George Sanders?"

I bowed, slightly.

"Saw you in a picture once," he went on. "Something of *Sunnybrook Farm*, think it was. My wife said you got what was coming to you."

"*Rebecca*," I corrected him. "Just that, with two *c*'s. Not of Sunnybrook Farm. Du Maurier, you know."

"Do what?" the sheriff asked.

I smiled tolerantly.

Callahan beetled his brows at me. He had decided that he didn't like me. He made this evident. "What

I've heard of you, you're a kind of shady character. Where you from? You got a funny accent."

"If you mean where was I born—Russia."

"Oh," he said. It was easy to see what he thought of Russia.

Lamar James pushed him aside. "You're getting nowhere, Jerry. How do you know that wasn't the murder weapon, Mr. Sanders?"

I smiled with a confidence I didn't feel. I began to improvise, and directed my remarks at Callahan. He was the man in authority, and I wanted him to clear out, so that Sammy and I could go to work on the problem of the missing guns. If Lamar James stayed here and nosed around, he might turn up a few facts that would be embarrassing to me.

"Suppose you shot the man, Sheriff?" I began.

"I wasn't even here," he bristled.

"Yes, I know. But suppose. The next act would be to hide the gun. Now where can you hide anything out there?" I waved at the valleys and dunes of sand, cosmic wrinkles in the Earth's ancient skin.

"You could hide a whole city in one of them dunes," the sheriff said.

"Could you, though?" I objected, wondering what I was really getting at. "With three hundred persons fluttering about, would you take such a chance in broad daylight? If you left the immediate vicinity, at least a few people would be likely to see you. No, you wouldn't hide the gun out there, Sheriff. You'd put it where nobody could observe you, and where nobody could find it. And you'd create the opportunity by planting another gun where it *could* be found, to divert attention from your act. This gun that you have found is a false clue, a red herring, a plant, a decoy. That's pretty obvious, don't you think?"

The sheriff simulated thoughtfulness. "Could be," he admitted.

"And you will find, when your ballistics expert examines the slug," I said impressively, "that it was *not* fired from this gun. It came from an entirely different make. This gun is a Colt thirty-eight, and the bullet was fired from a Smith and Wesson special."

"Baloney!" Callahan said. "You can't tell that by lookin' at the hole."

"Why not? Our friend Mr. James, with the micrometer mind, can tell at a glance that the slug is not a forty-five, that's a fairly incredible talent. Is it any more unbelievable that I should be able to name the make of gun?"

Lamar James cut in. "I believe it. You could call the turn under one condition—that you fired the shot."

"But I have an unbreakable alibi."

"Let's hear it!" he snapped.

"I was—" I began. I broke off as an embarrassing thought suddenly came into my mind. It was true that I was in camera range most of the time, but it was also true that I was carrying .38's. That fact would not escape James, for in the close-ups anyone could see that the gun which he had in custody was one of the guns I had fired in the scene. This would not necessarily indicate that I had shot Flynne, but it would certainly impair my claim that I had carried .45's.

"Are you charging me with murder?" I demanded.

"No," Lamar James said. "Not yet."

Riegleman broke in. "You'd better not. George is the star, and we've got to finish this picture. Do you know," he demanded of Sheriff Callahan, "how much it's costing to stand around here and gnaw the rag? Do you know how many hundred dollars an hour it costs?"

"Now, take it easy," placated the sheriff. "We're gonna let you go on as soon as we can."

Lamar James repeated, "Let's hear your alibi."

"I'll produce it when the time comes," I said aloofly.

He scowled, and Callahan scowled, but they let me get away with it.

"I'll remember that," James said darkly. "About the gun that shot him. Where do you think it's hidden?"

"I think we'll never find it," I said. "The killer has had plenty of time to hide the gun. The sand is soft, and it would be easy to dig a hole without arousing suspicion. Look."

I squatted and gazed out across the sand as if I were turning an important thought in my mind. To help me think, I scooped sand aimlessly. Presently I had a hole large and deep enough to bury a small badger. I dipped into my pocket for an imaginary gun, flipped it into the hole, and with my other hand scooped the hole full again.

"We could be standing on it here," I pointed out.

My point scored. "Then how," Callahan wailed, "are we gonna find the murderer? We can't rake over this whole area. We haven't got that kind of money in my office."

"We don't need the gun to find the murderer," I said coldly. "We find him by psychological detection. I'll tell you this much, the one we're looking for is brilliant, courageous, and shrewd. He is certain that he has covered his tracks. He won't run away. You might as well go check on that bullet. When you find that I'm correct, start looking for motives. That's the first step."

Callahan said, "Is that right, Lamar?"

"Yes," James answered. "That's right. Soon as the hearse gets here, we'll take off." He put his calm dark eyes on me. He ticked off fingers with, "One, that's not the murder weapon. Two, it was filled with blanks. Three, she wouldn't shoot a man in cold blood. That what you said?"

"Righto."

"I'm gonna want to see you," he said, "later."

"Come over to my trailer," I invited. "It's that big mahogany and chrome job down by the beach. I'll be in all evening."

He turned away. I stood undecided for a moment, almost weak with relief. The first round was mine. A remembered curiosity twinged, and I went over to Carla. I drew her off to one side.

"I'll buy you a coke," I said loudly, and led her toward the hot dog wagon.

"Thanks, George," she said in a low voice, "for rescuing me."

"The dogs were on your heels," I admitted. "But why were you scared? You didn't kill him."

She looked up at me. "How do you know?"

Here was the same poser. How *did* I know? I looked deeply into her dark eyes, and the reason came to me. It was not knowledge that I had, it was only emotion. Her eyes softened, and I touched her cheek with my hand.

I had known her casually for three or four years. We were friends. We had flirted some, light-hearted remarks tossed back and forth across a luncheon table at Romanoff's or the Derby.

Only that morning I'd been making love to her, madly, desperately. We had struck sparks from each other. I had caught her hand, and her eyes had smoldered. I'd kissed her, and her eyes had closed, dreamily. But that had been in a scene for *Seven Dreams,* and Riegleman had bawled for half a dozen retakes. Right now she was just a very nice kid that I liked and was a little worried about.

The Falcon, in a scene like this, alone with a beautiful woman—despite the unromantic setting of the hot dog wagon—would have done one of two things. He would have taken her in his arms and kissed her, ardently. Or, he'd have looked at her coldly and said, "Why did you kill Severance Flynne?"

I took a sip from my coke bottle. Then I said,

"Carla, why were you so scared at the sheriff's questions?"

There was a long pause before she answered, and I had a feeling she was counting ten. Finally she said, looking at her straw, "Don't be absurd."

"Don't be a liar," I said. "You were scared. Why?"

This time she counted to a hundred. Then she slid her coke bottle across the counter, looked at me, and said, "Sanders, you're a good guy, I like you. I'm in one hell of a jam here. Maybe you can tell me—" Suddenly her gorgeous mouth shut like a trap. Her eyes told me that someone was coming into hearing range.

It was Sammy. "Hi, Carla," he said. "Say, George, could you come and talk about the next scene? It needs a change, I think."

"Surely." I excused myself to Carla, and went along. "What's up?" I asked.

"Plenty," he said grimly, as we reached his office. "Come in and meet Listless."

Listless was a little blonde girl who sat in a huddle of misery in front of Sammy's desk. "She's in the wardrobe department," Sammy said. "Miss Nelson, Mr. Sanders."

I bowed. She said, "Hello," in a timid, frightened voice. She looked at Sammy.

That look said several things. It said that she had a head full of doughnut holes and a heart full of devotion to Sammy.

"Here," Sammy said, "is your person who is shrewd, brilliant, full of initiative and courage. You tell him, Listless."

She looked up at me, her great blue eyes glistening with imminent tears. "I was just trying to help," she snuffled.

"I'm sure you were," I said softly.

"I walked up here with Sammy," she went on,

"and he looked at that gun and said it was sure funny because he gave you another one and what did you do with it because it was worth a fortune. He said that strange gun didn't belong here and he wasn't going to trade a museum piece for modern junk. So then when I heard there'd been a murder and thought about what Sammy said about the gun and all I thought I'd help him. So I took both guns out of his desk and threw 'em away so the cops wouldn't find 'em on him. And now Sammy's mad at me."

She began to cry, gently, as if she didn't want to disturb anybody. Sammy and I just looked at each other.

Chapter Six

SHREWD, BRILLIANT, cunning, courageous. I'd had it all figured out. For some obscure reason, the murderer had taken the guns. We could expect something sensational in the way of developments. Oh, yes.

Listless continued to cry softly. Her problem was more serious to her than ours—Sammy was mad at her.

"I didn't *go* to do anything wrong," she said.

I put my hand on her head. "Where did you throw the guns, darling?"

She pointed a shaking finger. "Out there, on the other side of that big pile of sand."

"I wonder if anybody saw you."

"I don't think so," she said. "It was when everybody started down to the wagon to see what was going on. When I got back, they were still there. I didn't see anybody around here."

"Will you run along now, and let me and Sammy do some talking?"

She got up, dabbing at tears. She looked at Sammy.

"Are you still mad at me, Sammy?"

"Oh, hell," Sammy said wearily, "what's the use to be sore. I know you were trying to help. Listen, kid, don't do a thing on your own before you've asked me, will you? And don't say anything to anybody about this, huh?"

"I won't, Sammy. Honest."

"And don't wander around alone," I said. "Stay with people. We—well, I must confess that I haven't the foggiest notion of what we're up against, and until we find out, it may not be safe to boggle about."

Listless went out, and we sat silently for a while.

"George," Sammy said tentatively.

I gave him a three-quarter view of my face. I didn't actually look at him. "I know what you're going to say, Sammy. You're going to ask me to solve this crime in a hurry. You're going to point out that I have had a great deal of experience in the role of detective. You're going to mention my inventiveness. You're going to suggest that I pull a surprise out of my hat, something that will bewilder the murderer and force him into an unwary move. You're going to say that I am really like the character I have portrayed, clever, shrewd, fearless."

"Well, George, I wasn't. I was just going to say that you've been kind of dopey on this so far, and maybe we just ought to tell that deputy sheriff what we know and let him work on it."

"Oh."

Poor Sammy. Dealer in the obvious. Now is forever, was the way he felt. He couldn't see that bad breaks over which I had no control had put me in a rather bad light. I was correct in theory, and I knew it. Was it my fault that Listless, in an orgy of adulation, had intervened? The murderer would have taken the guns if he'd known where they were. My deductions fitted the known facts. Could I be blamed if those facts had unsuspected ramifications?

"You had it all figured out," Sammy amplified. "But you had it figured out wrong. Maybe we ought to stop messing around."

"You don't know, Sammy. You don't know how hick policemen jump at conclusions. If we told them how we'd lied about the guns, they'd toss us both in jail, as accessories if nothing worse. We have withheld facts, and that action has aided the murderer. My private opinion is that they'd waste no more time on me. They'd charge me with murder, and give me the privilege of disproving it."

"Well, maybe. All right, then, why don't we just clam up? If we don't know from nothing, what could they do? They'd never find the gun, and it would go down as an unsolved crime. How about that?"

"But, Sammy!" I protested. "We just can't let a killer wander about. It isn't good citizenship."

"Lay off the lecture," Sammy said. "Besides, we're about to have company."

Our company was McGuire, head of props. He was like a short brown wire. He had a shrewd, wrinkled face and bright gray eyes. He came in smiling.

"I'd like to put those guns away," he said to Sammy. "We won't need 'em before tomorrow."

"I'll bring 'em over after a while," Sammy stalled. "We're working on a scene."

McGuire shrugged, and went away. Sammy frowned.

"We get deeper and deeper," he said. "What am I going to tell him? They were his responsibility."

"He'll pass the buck to you in case of trouble."

"What'll I tell the cops, then?" Sammy wailed. "Am I gonna say I gave you the guns, and I only got one back? That the other was in Carla's wagon, and you had a strange gun on you, a Smith & Wesson thirty-eight, just like the gun you claim is the murder weapon? My God, look where that puts you. You had this strange gun, and now it's gone."

"That," I said gently, "is what I pointed out to you. The inference is so obvious that they'd take their minds off the actual murderer. We must keep quiet, if we expect to find the killer."

"George, I don't like it. I don't want to be mixed up in it."

"You *are* mixed up in it, though," I said reasonably. "It was you who gave me the signal to say nothing when you lied about the thirty-eights. Besides, Sammy, I need you."

"Oh, hell!" Sammy growled. "Why do people have to make friends? If a friend asks you for help, you've got to play ball or be a heel. And heels get along pretty well. There's a lot of 'em in our business, doing all right."

"Thanks, Sammy. I knew you'd see it my way."

"I don't see it your way at all. But what else can I do?" He glanced out the door. "Oh, God, here comes somebody else. You'd think this was the men's can."

The bearded extra who had asked Riegleman about his place in the scheme of things came to the door. He stabbed Sammy with his sharp black eyes.

"Mr. Riegleman told me, sir, to ask you."

"He would," Sammy muttered. "Just pack up your troubles and drop 'em in my lap."

The man waited for Sammy to go on. The silence got a trifle embarrassing.

"Well?" Sammy finally snapped.

"I'm sorry," the man apologized. "I did not comprehend that you had finished. I am trying to ascertain the reason for my presence here."

"Did it ever occur to you," Sammy asked gently, "that we're shooting a picture?"

"Yes," the man said with dignity, "I understand that. But this strange series of events which began in Hollywood has me somewhat bewildered. You see, my agent told me to report to your studio. When I did, I was told to go to Gate Seven. Gate Seven bore a sign: 'Beards.' The man inside took one look at me and told me to report Monday morning ready to come here. Why?"

"You're getting your fifteen dollars a day," Sammy snapped. "What do you want, a supporting role? Are you kicking about the dough?"

"Dear me," the man said, "as much as that? Then I have no complaint on the score of remuneration. But I still do not understand—"

"It will all be made clear," Sammy said. "Just keep yourself in readiness. You'll get your orders."

"I see." A reflective pause. "I—see." He didn't.

That was very clear. "Thank you." He went away, tall, lean, stooped, his head shaking.

"You meet some funny ones," Sammy said, looking after him. "Now, where were we?"

"I want you to do something, Sammy. I want you to get the film that was being shot while Flynne was being murdered and bring it over to my trailer. Tonight, before they ship it back to the studio to be developed."

Sammy's eyes went round with scandalized horror. "George! The master film! Undeveloped stock! You can't do that. It would be like asking Congress to loan you the original Declaration of Independence."

"You want to trap the murderer, don't you?"

"Not under those conditions. I'd rather forget about him. If Riegleman caught me, he'd tear my hide off with his teeth."

"Look, Sammy. The cameras recorded all the action. That film will furnish alibis for several hundred persons. If we give out the news that we have it and know that it contains a very important clue, the murderer will have to get the film and destroy it. Wouldn't you, if you were the murderer?"

"Not the master film, George! My God, that's sacrilege!"

"The murderer won't see it that way, Sammy."

"Then he's a dirty rat. Look, that was a swell scene this morning. We can't take a chance on getting the film destroyed. We'd have to shoot it over, and maybe do retakes. That costs *money*, George! Listen, I've worked with Riegleman for a year. When he spends a nickel, he's got to have an aspirin. You'd think he raised that buffalo from a calf."

"Only if it's someone else's money," I reminded Sammy. "That's what's made him a success as a producer, remember. A successful producer gets to be a rich man. And Riegleman—"

"A modest little home in the country," Sammy said softly, and grinned.

I repressed a grin. "Let's don't be unkind," I said.

"Twenty-six rooms and nine baths," Sammy murmured. "Two swimming pools—one, of course, for the servants. A private shooting gallery where he can show off his fancy marksmanship. Remember the time he made a bet with the bit player who'd once been a bodyguard for Capone?"

"He won it, didn't he?" I said. "Wish I'd been there." It must have been a memorable evening. A deck of cards tacked up on the target, and Riegleman and the ex-bodyguard playing poker by shooting at the cards. "Anyway, why shouldn't he have the kind of modest little house he wants?"

"If he ever gets it paid for," Sammy said, "he'll trade it in as down payment on another modest little home. This one with a private golf course and a polo field."

"All right, he's ambitious," I retorted. "It's his money. Let's veer back to business. About this film." I paused. "As a matter of fact, Sammy, you might say I was doing this for Riegleman."

Sammy blinked. "Come again?"

"I'm trying to save money, Sammy."

"How?"

"Suppose the sheriff makes us stay here until the crime is solved. You and I know that would take him forever. And the costs would pile up every day. Now, if we clean up the case tonight, we can hand him his murderer and go on with the picture. We don't lose any time."

Sammy thought about it. "You think you can clean it up?"

"Tonight."

"Well—" Presently, he heaved to his small feet. "All right, but I hope to God you know what you're doing."

"While you're getting the film," I said, "I'll drive a couple of stakes so that when they're lined up they'll direct us to the dune where Listless threw the guns. If all this stuff is moved to another location, we'd have no landmark. And we can't go out looking for the guns now. We'd be seen. Not that I think we'll need them, anyway. But best not to chance it."

"I'll need the other gun in that museum pair," Sammy said. "We'd better find it." He groaned. "Priceless guns, undeveloped stock. Somebody's gonna catch up with us. God, what a mess! Good-by, George. If I get caught, plant a rose for me somewhere."

I sat for some time, thinking. I tried to drum up a little self-contempt. We were motivated by strictly personal considerations. I wanted to catch the murderer to forestall personal difficulty. I doubted that even I could explain to the sheriff how I was innocent in this mixed-up mess. And Sammy was going along in the hope of getting the picture finished on schedule. Neither of us thought about Severance Flynne.

As I went out to get a hammer and a couple of stakes, I resolved that I would find out something about Flynne. I must know his background to some extent in order to ascribe a motive for murder. Then, when I could define a motive, all I needed was the person at whose feet it could be laid, and I would have the killer. Very simple.

As I drove the last stake, the killer would have erased me if I hadn't put my back into the last blow. I put my back into it, which saved my life. My head was in motion. I knew, in a fragment of time between light and darkness, that I had been hit a terrific blow on the head.

Chapter Seven

I CAME TO in the first-aid trailer, with the burn of raw brandy in my throat, and sacrificial drums in my head.

Sammy, Paul, Riegleman, and Lamar James were there, crowded so close together that they were just a tangle of arms and legs.

"I know where I am," I said, "but what year is it?"

"You've only been out a few minutes," Lamar James said. "Somebody smacked you with a hammer. It wasn't a solid blow, it just tore up a strip of scalp. Otherwise, they'd be making out entrance papers for you—somewhere."

They all eyed me as if I were in a glass case, with a printed placard: "George Sanders, good, if battered, specimen. From the *Seven Dreams* collection."

Lamar James said, "What were you doing out there?"

I had no answer ready other than to say I was staking a mining claim. I hoped Sammy had. I said, "Let Sammy tell you. I don't feel like talking."

"Why?" James demanded. "There's no concussion. You're not really hurt."

"Somebody left an old cement mixer in my skull."

He grinned, put his dark eyes on Sammy. "We were talking about the next scene," Sammy said glibly. "George wanted some changes in it. So he drove a couple of stakes to illustrate his point."

"That was a lot of work just to illustrate a point," James said. "I felt those stakes. You could snub a landslide with 'em."

"I got carried away," I said.

"Yes, and it took all four of us, you big oaf," Sammy said.

Riegleman and Paul looked at me with disbelief. They knew the script. They couldn't figure how a couple of stakes could fit into the next scene, changes or no. Neither could I. I closed my eyes, and Lamar James pried at them with questions.

"Did you see anybody?"

"No."

"Hear anybody?"

"No."

"It looks like an attempt to kill you," James said. "Why would anyone want to kill you?"

"I haven't the faintest notion." I opened my eyes. "I thought you and the sheriff were going."

"I was on my way," he said, "when Sammy found you and yelled for help."

I closed my eyes again. I didn't want Sammy to see the glint of suspicion. He had been nearest to me at the time. He could have done it. But I had waited for a few moments after he left me. Even so, he could have gone to the lab and returned in plenty of time.

I gave it up for the time being. "What now?"

Riegleman said, "I'll tell you what now. We do no more work today. You've been knocked for six and need rest. What's more," he said to James, "George must have a bodyguard. If the killer has selected him as the next victim, we must protect him until the picture is finished. He is the star."

I grinned at him, a little sourly. "Let's not endanger the picture, by all means."

"I didn't mean it so callously, George," Riegleman apologized. "But the picture *is* a big consideration. We can't jeopardize our investment."

"This isn't getting anywhere," Lamar James broke in. "We won't get anywhere until we get some more information." He turned to Riegleman. "Tell everybody—and I mean everybody—not to leave town."

He shouldered his way out. I sat up. The brandy was a warm glow in my stomach now. I felt middling well.

Riegleman turned to Sammy. "Assign a couple of good men to stay with George." He turned to me. "Don't go anywhere without them."

"All right," I said.

Sammy waited for me, outside. "I've got the film, George. What about this bodyguard?"

"Not yet," I told him. "I need to find out a few things. I wish I knew where Flynne was quartered."

"I thought you might want to know, so I looked

it up. He was in room fourteen at the Olsen Hotel."

"Then I'll take off. You bring the film over to my trailer, and I'll join you there."

I pushed my convertible at top speed across the sandy road until I reached the highway, then roared the three miles into Royalton. I strolled into the hotel, happy to find no desk clerk, and located Flynne's room.

If I could get some idea of Flynne as a person, his background, habits, and so on, I would be better equipped to work on possible motive, and the one person it fitted.

His door was unlocked, and I went in. The place had been cleaned, the bed made, and his personal belongings put neatly away. These consisted of clothes, a few pipes, a pound can of cheap tobacco, and a carton of cigarettes. Nothing in the dresser drawers was any more personal than this. The mattress of his bed seemed to hide nothing. The porcelain pitcher had water in it, the washbowl was empty. A few clothes hung in the closet, and the pockets were empty except for a couple of ticket stubs from Grauman's Chinese and a fountain pen. On the bed table was a litter of match folders, a couple of pencils, a pottery ash tray, and an empty glass.

Nothing to indicate that this was Flynne's room. No old letters, no initialed handkerchiefs, nothing. A handsome pigskin bag in the closet was also bare of initials, and empty. Empty, that is, at first glance. In one of the flat compartments I found a newspaper clipping.

It was from a clipping service, but the name of the

service had been torn from the pink label pasted to the clipping itself. This read:

TRAGEDY IN MONDESLEY

Lord Hake, member of the House from Burnham and head of one of our oldest families, died of pneumonia Friday midnight in his home, the Woods.

His eldest son, Harry, met his death almost simultaneously in Mondesley when his Daimler ran over an embankment. It is believed that he was hurrying to his father's bedside and lost his way in a heavy fog.

The clipping, which was from an English newspaper, continued with a two-paragraph history of the family. It was all very dull. It meant absolutely nothing to me.

A knock on the door sent the clipping into my pocket and me into the clothes closet. The knock was repeated; after a moment, the door opened stealthily and Wanda Waite came into the room.

She had on a short white dress, her blonde hair was becomingly tumbled. Her lovely long legs were bare and brown. I appreciated the picture she made before I realized that her face was set, grim, and pale.

She looked about the room with frightened eyes, and went swiftly to the bed table. She stood between me and the table, with her back to me, and I strained my eyes through the crack in the closet door to see what she was doing there.

She seemed to be handling and examining everything on the table. Was she searching for something? Was she finding something and putting it in her purse? I couldn't tell. I could see her pick up the empty glass and put it down. She moved to the dresser, picked up and examined the porcelain pitcher and washbowl. She stood for a moment with her hand resting on the metal footboard of the bed. Then suddenly she turned and almost ran from the room. She closed the door softly behind her and went away.

The litter on the table looked undisturbed to me. Match folders, pencils, ash tray, empty glass. The match folders all bore the insignia of the Royalton Hardware Co., Inc. I shut my eyes and tried to remember if I had seen a different folder among them. I couldn't.

Had she put something in her purse? Nothing seemed to be gone from the table. What had she been searching for? Most important of all, had she found it? I began to feel dizzy.

I decided I had better go away. Lamar James would certainly be along soon, not to mention nameless persons who might wander in as Wanda had. This was no time for deduction. I went away with the clipping in my pocket.

Among the gadgets I had installed in my trailer is a photoelectric cell which throws a beam across the door. It is connected to the lights, so that when I set a foot across the threshold the lights snap on. I don't have to fumble around in the dark for a switch.

I plugged a 300-watt daylight bulb, with a reflector behind it, into the light circuit and unscrewed all the wall lamps. I focused this searchlight on the door, at about the height of an adult's eyes. If anyone came through the door at night, he should be instantly blinded. I tested my work, and it was good.

Then Sammy arrived with the film, carrying it gingerly, and wearing the expression of a man who has just made off with the Mona Lisa.

"Don't worry," I reassured him. "It'll be safe with me."

I looked at the flat shiny can. A harmless looking thing, but possibly containing the clue to a murderer. Or the proof of someone's innocence. I handled it with care.

"Too bad we're not in Hollywood," I mused. "I could develop this and make a print of it, and we could look at it."

"It would take more than that to get my mind off my worries," Sammy groaned.

"That film probably does contain a fine collection of clues," I told him. "Perhaps if we could see it, we wouldn't have to set a trap."

Sammy squinted at me. "Oh." He was silent for a moment. "It'll prove you didn't shoot him. I remember. You were facing the camera in that scene. Flynne was behind you, in the crowd."

"If you could only remember where everyone else was at the time," I said, "it might save a lot of trouble."

"I couldn't be watching everything," Sammy said, almost apologetically. "I didn't know there was going to be a murder."

"No. Only the murderer knew that. And that reminds me of something. If the murderer was in the scene, he'd know that the camera would record his every action. He couldn't take such a chance. It must have been someone behind the cameras."

Sammy sighed. "So that leaves the sound men, cameramen, grips, props, the boom crew, Paul, Riegleman, me, the script girl, the wardrobe people, and the cook and two waitresses in the commissary."

"We can eliminate most of those, Sammy. Most of them were busy."

"Who wasn't?" Sammy objected. "Everybody was busy."

"Yes, it seems so."

"Maybe it was an accident, George. Maybe ·that screwball deputy is nuts on that thirty-eight deal."

"Then where did the extra gun come from, the Smith & Wesson?"

"Yeah," he said gloomily, "that's right."

"And why did somebody bonk me on the conk?"

"Yeah," he said in the same gloomy tone.

"I've thought of something," I said. "You remembered that when Flynne was shot, I was facing the camera. If the shot came from behind the camera, it had to come from almost directly in front of me. Therefore, I must have been looking in the direction of the murderer. Maybe he—or she—thinks I saw him. That would be plenty of motive to kill me."

Sammy's face brightened. "Say, maybe you've got something there."

"Well, don't be so cheerful about it. Here's what

we'll do next. We'll go out and spread the tidings. We'll say that I have the film because I know it contains a vital clue to the murder. You don't know what it is, and I'm not saying. Suppose you tell a few members of the technical group, and a few of the administrative. I'll tell a few of the actors. Everybody ought to hear about it inside an hour. Then we'll see what happens."

"What about this film?"

"We'll hide it. Rather, I'll hide it. You run along. I'll come later."

"Why?" Sammy demanded. "Don't you trust me?"

"Of course," I said lightly. "I know *you* didn't do it. If you don't know where the film is, nobody will trap you into any admission, or try to beat one out of you. It's for your own protection."

"How about your protection?" Sammy said. "If Riegleman finds out that I didn't provide a bodyguard for you, I'll be in the soup." He paused. "What I really mean is, if you know where the film is, what's to prevent somebody from beating the hell out of you?"

"I am prepared to defend myself. I have a gun. I'll take it with me."

Sammy hunched his round shoulders and left. I stood in the door and watched him for several hundred yards of moonlight until he reached his coupe.

I turned out the lamp and made a survey. Between my trailer and the surf, a few hundred feet distant, the hard sand was clearly lighted by a lopsided moon. I could see anybody coming from that direction. This also held true on the town side. Bare sand surrounded me. The town was marked by a faint glow half a mile away, and that glow would silhouette anybody coming from that direction.

Down the beach was a jumble of boulders casting weird shadows. I might be approached from there with impunity.

I cut in the photoelectric-searchlight circuit and sat down to wait. Somebody, I felt sure, would come through that door before long.

Time creeps in the dark, with no sense of passage. It fumbles blindly for the next position on the clock, and though each tick is a measurable footstep, it seems never to get its feet off the ground. And so I sat for a couple of years, ears strained for visitors.

My thoughts came to a head. In one lordly gesture, I lopped from the list of suspects all and sundry who had galloped or grimaced before the camera. The killer *must* have been behind it.

Very soon now, the killer would have heard Sammy's fiction. So, inevitably the killer would come through my door to see what he could see. My low cunning gave me warmth in the darkness that was growing chill.

Sharpened by tension, my ears caught a sound outside. It grew louder. Footsteps crunched carelessly through sand. Yes, the killer would come in that fashion, openly. For he believed he was unsuspected, and would no doubt have a rational story if he should be seen. I took my small pistol from the window seat beside me and pointed it in the general direction of the door.

The searchlight snapped on with the opening of the door.

"Don't move!" I said. "I've got you covered."

My agent, Melva Lonigan, blinked blindly in the glare, and shivered. "Thank God for that," she said. "I'd have frozen in another minute!"

Chapter Eight

I FLICKED THE SWITCH and plunged us into darkness. "Come over here and sit down," I hissed. "And be quiet."

"But why?" she demanded.

"I'm waiting for a murderer. Let's hope he didn't see that light."

"I hope Fred saw it, George. He wouldn't like our being unchaperoned in the dark."

"Oh, Lord," I said. "Fred too. With three of us in here, the murderer couldn't get in anyway. If you'll kick at the door we'll have some light."

The searchlight blazed again, and Melva shielded her eyes. "Do we have to have that beacon?"

I fixed up some bearable lights and glared at her. "I suppose there is some explanation for your impeding the wheels of justice. And why did you come out without a coat? That dress, what there is of it, may be suitable for a warm night in Hollywood, but you're three hundred miles north, and on the coast."

"We made it in five hours," she said smugly. "Fred drives like a fiendish angel. Or vice versa. Have you got an old blanket or something, or a stove? If you cut my throat, I'd bleed crimson icicles."

I turned on my electric heater, and she stood beside it. "Mmmm! That feels good!"

Shoes crunched on sand outside, and Fred Forbes came in. He arranged his horse face in mock suspicion. "The lights go out, the lights come on, the lights go dim. What goes?"

"George has another invention," Melva said. "You kick a hole in space, and there is light. It probably won't make any money, but it's cute—in a blinding sort of way."

Fred grinned. "I never have been able to decide whether he's trying to be a poor man's Edison, or just Don Ameche." *Mr. Ameche played Alexander Graham Bell in The story of Alexander Graham Bell, (1939) (See p. 10 footnote)*

"Don't scoff," Melva admonished. "Everybody laughed at the Wright brothers, remember. Though I must admit," she added thoughtfully, "they never tried to hook a fire siren up to a mouse trap. George, I'm awfully glad that gadget didn't work well. Aside from problems with the SPCA, think of the mouse. A great big THING screaming in its poor little ears after it was trapped."

"The one I liked," Fred said dreamily, "was that radio self-tuner that was allergic to the human voice, and switched automatically to music when the commercials came on. That would have been nice—if it had worked."

"Your bargain-counter wit," I said, "is excruciating, and I mean painful. Not all my inventions were failures."

"Law of averages," Fred said. "It's with you all the

time. How's that telephone gadget coming on, the one with a loudspeaker and mike in every room?"

"None of your business. Sit down. When you stand, you look as if you're falling apart."

He grinned. "I am kind of loose jointed, I guess. Listen, I got a great idea. We give out that you're going to—"

"We will not!" Melva cut in. "George, you've got to stay out of—"

"Stay out?" Fred cried. "Stay *out?* The opportunity of a—"

"The opportunity to get himself—" Melva interrupted.

"Be still!" I said. "I feel like an old bone between you. What, if anything, is this all about?"

Melva waved Fred to silence. "I'll tell it. We heard, about three o'clock this afternoon, that somebody had got himself killed. So we came—I, to protect you; Fred, to ruin you."

"If you'd switch roles, I'd have more fun," I said. "I don't need protection."

"Then where did you get that bandage?" Melva demanded. "What's under it?"

"A lumpy head, darling. The murderer bopped me."

Melva gave a stricken moan. "Oh, George!"

"I wasn't hurt very badly," I reassured her.

"Thank God for that," she said with deep feeling. "If you get knocked off, I might as well go out of the agency business."

"Your solicitude," I told her, "is a thing of terrible beauty."

She pointed a stern finger at me. "You stay out of this murder, you hear? I can't afford it."

Fred said, "But—"

Melva cut him off with a savage gesture. She directed slit-eyed suspicion at me. "Are you playing detective on this?"

"I'm not playing," I said bitterly.

"Then I'm going to stay right here and see that you keep hands off," she said grimly. "Listen, do you know what happens to smarties who look for murderers? They find 'em, sometimes, only they never know about it. I am not going to let you get yourself killed. That's final."

"What have you found out so far, George?" Fred asked.

"Whatever it is," Melva broke in, "he's forgotten. Look, Georgie, you came to me only a few days ago saying you'd never take another role as a gumshoe. But I knew different. It's in your blood. When I heard about this guy—what *is* his name, anyway?—getting killed, I knew you'd be in the thick of it. So I'm here to tell you you can't go back on your word."

Fred took her by the shoulders and pushed her onto the window seat. Neither his action nor expression invited any protest from her. "You stay there," he said. "You be quiet." He turned to me, ignoring her. "Here's my idea. You *can* solve this thing, can't you?" He put a hand tightly over Melva's mouth as she started to say something.

"I'd have had it wrapped up if you two had stayed where you belonged," I said. "God knows what will happen now."

"You're on the track of the killer, then?"

"Or vice versa," I said, touching the bandage.

Melva bit Fred's hand. He jerked it away. "That's what I mean," she said. "Are you trying to put me out of business?" she demanded angrily. "George got mixed up in this thing and he got his head cracked. He's got to get out."

"I can't," I said. "I'm a suspect."

"Oh, Lord!" Melva moaned. "There goes your career!"

"If I could have a word," I said. "That is, if you don't mind too much. I've been under the impression that both of you are working for me, though I am sometimes confused on that point. At any rate, your emoluments are deducted or deductible from my income tax, and I think that makes you, legally, my employees. As your boss, then, I have an order. Scram!"

"Not until we know what goes on," Melva said firmly. "You'll have to throw us out bodily. If you do, I'll have you arrested for assault."

"You're trespassing on my property," I pointed out.

She pulled her skirt up above her knees and arranged her beautiful legs in a witness-chair pose. "I was just bringing him some calves-foot jelly," she said to an imaginary panel of twelve, "and he attacked me." To me, sweetly, "Do you think they'd believe me—or you? Which?"

"I am not amused by idle threats."

"You think they're idle? Try putting me out!"

"She means it, George," Fred said. "She had me arrested once. She gave me a cigarette case, and I gave it to my baby brother. That made her mad, and she claimed I stole it from her and sold it to him. She'd have had him pinched as a receiver of stolen goods if he hadn't been under age. So don't give her an opening."

I went to the door. "I'm going out. I'm hungry. You two can stay here and vegetate if you like."

They were after me like fox hounds. "We accept with pleasure," Melva said. "It's a long time since you took us to dinner. Shall we go in your car or ours?"

"Going out?" a voice asked from the door. Lamar James lounged there, eyeing us steadily. He came inside. "I'm glad I caught you," he said to me.

"Caught him?" Melva echoed. "He didn't do anything. He was with me all the time."

James ran an appreciative eye over her. "Who are you, Miss?"

I made the introductions. "My agent, and press agent," I explained.

James nodded. "How did you know Mr. Sanders was in a jam?" he asked Melva.

"When murder comes," she said, "can George be far behind?"

James grinned briefly. He looked at me. "I came over for our little talk. I'd like to ask you a few questions."

"Good," I said. I turned to Fred and Melva. "I'm happy that you dropped in. I'll see you in Hollywood."

"Oh, no, you don't!" Melva said. She turned to James and added, "We have a considerable investment wrapped up in this piece of property, and we intend to see that he stays intact. He's no good subdivided."

James's eyes sparkled a little. "I'm getting tired," he said levelly, "of this Hollywood attitude. Can't you people get it through your heads that a man has been killed? It's a human life gone. No matter who or what he was, it was his life and he wanted it. But—" He paused and ran a hand over his hair. "I never saw such an outfit. Mr. Riegleman is worried about his shooting schedule. What's his name—Paul—is afraid he'll lose his job because a stranger sneaked in with somebody else's work permit. That fat guy, Sammy, tells one lie after another. And Mr. George Sanders gets in my hair at every turn. Meanwhile, a man is dead! Maybe he wanted to live, just the same as you. Can you get that through your heads?"

The silence was uncomfortable.

"I'm sorry," Melva murmured. She paused and said apologetically, "It's only natural to think of your own interests."

"Yeah, all right. Well, Mr. Sanders, what about these two? Will you talk in front of 'em?"

I sighed. "Show me an alternative."

"I could arrest you," he said flatly, "and we could talk in your cell."

"Arrest me for what?"

"We'll come to that later."

"They'd better stay, then," I decided. "I may need

a friend on the outside. What do you want to know?"

"Let's sit down," he said. "Instead of standing here like prize-fighters waiting for the bell."

There were barely enough seats. Melva ran her eyes around the crowded space. "Hang out the S.R.O. sign, Fred."

James flicked her a glance, and she colored under it. "Now," he said to me. "You say that Miss Folsom couldn't have shot Flynne. How do you know?"

"She isn't the type," I said.

James shook his dark head doggedly. "That doesn't go with me. There isn't any 'type', and you know it. You're holding back information, Mr. Sanders, and I want to know what it is."

"Don't be ridiculous," I said. "I've known Carla for several years, and I know she hasn't the capacity for murder. She's a very sweet, gentle person."

"Look, Mr. Sanders, I know you're no dope," James said patiently. "That girl is scared. You knew it, and you rushed in to defend her. I didn't go on questioning her, because I got lots of time. I thought I'd wait, and see what happened. But I got to thinking it over, and I knew you'd have kept out of it if you didn't have some reason to believe she didn't fire the shot. I mean an actual, concrete reason. What is it?"

"My faith in her," I said gravely.

"Galahad!" Melva muttered. It was a bad word in her mouth.

I continued to hold tight. "I have nothing else to say," I told him.

"All right. We'll lay that thought away, and take up

another one. You said the slug came out of a Smith
& Wesson thirty-eight. You can't tell that by looking
at the hole."

"Why not?" I demanded. "Remember, I found the
body. I could study the wound while it was fresh."

"What made you think it was a Smith & Wesson?"

He had me there. Unless I could read the trade
mark, I didn't know a Smith & Wesson from a
Webley. "It's very simple," I said. "The characteristics of small arms are definite, according to make and
type. I have made some study of these, in my own
modest way. As a result of my research, I was able to
identify the make of weapon."

James snorted. "Look, you're going to have to tell
all this to a coroner's jury tomorrow. So you'd better
make a better story of it than that. Because, you see,
I'm the coroner, too."

"If I tell the truth, I have nothing to fear."

"Yeah, *if*. Tell me one difference in the ballistics
characteristics between a slug from a Colt thirty-
eight Special and a Smith & Wesson same."

"If I so choose," I said, unfairly, "I can order you
out. I needn't talk to you. I'm not under arrest."

He sighed. "Yes, you are too under arrest. I hoped
I wouldn't have to do this. But I'm trying to nab the
person who killed Flynne. I haven't any interest in
amateurs who want to show off for the newspapers,
which the presence of your press agent indicates. I
hoped you'd tell me what you know, because you
know some things I don't. But since you're so trouble-
some, you're under arrest."

"On what charge?" I asked quietly.

"Illegal parking," he said. "We got a city ordinance that says nobody can establish living quarters on our beach. Sure, you can be bailed out or pay a ten-dollar fine, but not before tomorrow. Because Judge Guilding has gone home, and he doesn't like being disturbed. In the meantime, you and I can have a little heart to heart talk for a few hours. Come on!"

Chapter Nine

H̲E̲ ̲D̲I̲D̲N̲'̲T̲ ̲R̲E̲A̲L̲L̲Y̲ ̲W̲A̲N̲T̲ to arrest me. That made us even, I didn't really want to be arrested.

This may sound over-fastidious, but there were other, and important considerations. I am no believer in truth prevailing over all. History is smudged with wars between the true and the false, and you may toss a coin for the winner. So, although I had not laid Severance Flynne dead in the dust, I was not completely certain that I could convince Lamar James or a jury of that fact.

I knew that I should have followed my first impulse and told the truth about the guns. Now that Sammy and Listless had further complicated the situation, I didn't dare.

Of course, when the reel of film was developed, it would prove me innocent. But in the meantime, if Lamar James got me alone in a small cell, he could take all night for an interview. My idea of a big night is not to spend it in a small town jail.

Besides, there was the trap I'd set for the murderer. It had been interfered with enough already.

I looked at Lamar James. "I see no need to toss me

in the tank," I said. "All you want is conversation anyway. Suppose we go to dinner and have a nice quiet chat."

James colored. "You can't bribe me."

"Does asking a man to dinner constitute an attempt at bribery?" I demanded, with cold dignity.

"In this case," he said steadily, "yes."

He had me there. I wouldn't answer his questions, and he wouldn't go to dinner. This deadlock brought a strained silence.

Fred broke it with, "There are three of us, George. We can teach this hick cop a lesson. I don't like this illegal parking gag. I couldn't make a country weekly with the yarn. Now if he wants to make it a murder charge—"

"Stop dreaming headlines," Melva commanded. She turned to James. "You can't put him in jail. He has to work tomorrow, and he'd look like the devil if he didn't get any sleep. We're not going to let you put him in jail."

James paid no attention to them. "Come on, Mr. Sanders."

"I'd like very much to have a word about my own welfare," I said. "If you—all of you—hadn't come charging in here like the Light Brigade, I'd have had your murderer all wrapped up by now." A thought struck me. "Not necessarily yet, however. Look here, if you'll all be quiet for a few minutes, we'll test it. I laid a trap for the murderer tonight, and maybe it isn't too late to set it again. Will you agree to try it?" I asked James.

"What kind of a trap?"

I explained that Sammy was out spreading a story. "It doesn't matter what the story is," I said. "It's enough to know that it was designed to draw the murderer here. It's possible, of course, that he has been scared off by the lights and the convention we've been holding, but it's also possible that he hasn't started yet. All of you sit quietly while I put out the lights."

Without waiting for permission, I brought darkness again and cut the searchlight back into the circuit. "And don't breathe heavily," I said.

"I'm between you and the door, Sanders," James said. "Don't make any breaks."

"That's a lovely picture," Melva murmured. "George resisting arrest on a parking charge, and getting shot for it. Mr. James, if you impair his earning capacity one cent, you'll be combing me out of your hair from now on."

"Shoot him where it won't show," Fred said.

"Be quiet!" I hissed.

All we needed was a Fuller Brush man, and I hadn't any doubt we'd have one before the night was out. If many more people got the itch to visit me, I'd have to butter a shoe horn.

I tried to put myself in the murderer's place, there in the dark. He had shot Flynne and planted the gun on me. The next development was almost inevitable: the gun would be found on me, I would be arrested, and the issue so confused that the killer might escape notice. But Sammy had taken the gun, and the investigation shot off on an unforeseen tangent. What had the murderer done then? As nearly as I could see, he hadn't done anything. It was as if he had done a job, and had no further interest in the matter. He dusted his hands of the affair. But his interest had revived when I was driving in that stake.

Why?

Unless the killer was Sammy, he couldn't have known what I was doing. He couldn't have known that Listless had thrown the murder weapon away. Why, then, did he bludgeon me? Was my record as a screen detective so firmly fixed in his mind that he identified the reel man with the real?

It could be. He could watch my reactions from the time I discovered the body. He could see me uncover the gun in the wagon; he could listen to my fairy tale to James and Callahan. He knew that Sammy knew we had an odd gun. He could see me and Sammy in whispered colloquy.

Then he could remember: as *The Saint* and/or *Falcon* I had been attracted by crimes cast not in the common mold. And, as those super-sleuths, I always brought the culprit to bay. Justice prevailed, the innocent were exonerated, and the maiden who thought I was wonderful continued to think I was wonderful as her growing eyes faded into "THE END."

Watching my actions, and remembering my scripted triumphs, the killer might easily have decided that I was up to no good for him.

The question now was whether he had already been scared away by the lights and voices, or whether he would arrive in search of the film. It was a psychological certainty that he would make an effort to destroy the film. He had to, so he thought, for it contained something highly significant.

All we had to do, then, was wait. And if he didn't show up tonight, we could arrange another trap later.

Provided, of course, that I could stay out of jail.

Above the slight sounds of our breathing and shifting, and the surf's whispered commands for silence, I heard a scuffing beyond the door. It was as if somebody had sneaked up to the trailer and now stood first on one foot and then on the other in indecision. This didn't fit into my earlier conception of the murderer. He should have come openly. But then, I reflected, I hadn't been correct on anything so far, except in insisting that Flynne's death wasn't accidental.

The others heard it, too. All breathing ceased, and I hoped they wouldn't hold their breaths too long. If everyone gasped for new breath at the same instant, whoever was outside would wonder how that steam engine had got in here.

But the door, softly, softly, swung outward. Silhouetted amorphously against the moonlighted sand outside was a tall, slim figure. Her foot intercepted the photo-electric beam, and the daylight bulb gave us a vision.

Wanda Waite had changed clothes again. She was in a shining black satin sheath and a black fur. Her hair was sleeked back over her ears. All she needed was a jade cigarette holder to double for the fascinating spy whom everybody suspected from the first reel. Even as she stood bewildered and blinking in the brilliance, she was an exciting pillar of intrigue.

I fixed the lights, and Wanda examined us with defiant, if frightened, blue eyes. She gave Melva and Fred a frozen smile of recognition. She looked at me and James without expression, as she took a jade cigarette holder from her bag, fitted a cigarette into it, and waited for somebody to offer a light.

I did so, trying to analyze the expression in her eyes. It was a combination of terror and bravado. Then, suddenly, her eyes changed. Where they had been veiled a moment before, they became liquid. Fascinated, I let the match burn my fingers. I shook out the flame abstractedly without removing my gaze from hers.

Her eyes implored. None but the blind would believe that she had played a missionary's wife. None but the impervious would think of murder when she looked like that.

James, the impervious, said, "What are you doing here?"

She didn't shift her I-am-yours-forever look for a full half minute. Then she took her eyes from mine with an expression of infinite regret. She gave James a half smile that seemed to deplore but accept the inevitable. She shrugged her shoulders, gestured with the cigarette holder. James looked embarrassed. I felt my cheeks redden.

Melva said, "Cornfield, here we come!"

James repeated, "What are you doing here?"

Wanda's voice had an overtone of embarrassment, but was nonetheless loaded with husky implication. "*Must* I explain?"

James glanced at me. He didn't say anything, but envy showed near the surface.

Melva said nastily, "That's a motive for murder too, sometimes."

James blinked, and looked as if he were coming out of a dream. He turned to Wanda. "I want to know the truth," he said, with a kind of forced grimness.

She put a touch of sorrow in her eyes. "Would a woman make such an admission if it were false?"

"I don't know," James said dryly. "I've never been a woman." He turned to me. "This was your party."

I became Launcelot on a white charger. "I have no reason to doubt the truth of her statement," I said.

"Can't we go where there's more room?" Melva asked. "If any more gals come after you, we'll all be smothered in the crush."

Fred, I noticed, had been standing motionless, his mouth open, since Wanda had come in.

James refused to be sidetracked. "I'd like to have your fingerprints," he said to Wanda.

She was shocked. "Why?"

"I want 'em, that's all."

"The romantic cop," Melva murmured. "A souvenir!"

Wanda was frightened again. Her hands, clenched and shaking, opened to fumble with her bag. She took out her lipstick and began to take off the cap. It fell out of her hands.

James stooped to retrieve it. Wanda held out her hand, already forming a tight smile of thanks. But the deputy put the lipstick carefully in his pocket.

Wanda's hand began to shake again. "I'll have that, if you please."

"Later," James said. "Maybe." He went to the door. "This is evidence. Don't leave town." He went out.

A puzzled silence fell over us. Wanda was definitely in a blue funk. Melva eyed her curiously. Fred just eyed her.

"That," I said thoughtfully, "was one my script writers missed. A new way, to me, of getting reluctant fingerprints."

"What have I done now?" Wanda whispered. "I never meant to hurt anybody in my life, and now I'm being treated like a criminal."

She turned and ran from the trailer.

Chapter Ten

M ELVA SAID, "*That* left everybody standing on one foot!"

"What's that cop interested in Wanda for?" Fred asked.

"*Somebody* shot Severance Flynne," I pointed out. "It could have been Wanda."

"Was it?" Fred asked tensely.

"No. She didn't kill him."

"Then why don't you tell the cop?" Melva demanded. "He's wasting time on her if she's innocent."

"I'm not ready to tell him yet. I honestly believe that I should have trapped the killer here tonight if you two hadn't got the bright idea of dropping in. Now, we may as well go to dinner. The killer must have been scared off by this time."

Melva took up a position between me and the door. Hands on hips, she stood on widespread feet and glared at me. "So you're not ready to tell him! You listen to me, George Sanders. You give up any dopey ideas you may have about solving this murder. You're up here to make a picture, and if you don't do a good job I'll never be able to get you another big part. And

you can't do a good job of acting if you mess around
on this, aside from the fact that you may get yourself
killed. So you just run along and tell that cop what he
wants to know."

"He'd arrest me if I did."

"But why? You said you didn't kill him, didn't
you?"

"I didn't kill him," I said patiently, "and I think
I can prove it. But the very proof which I can offer
will incriminate me to some extent. It will probably
absolve me, but at the same time it will show that I
not only lied but that I have interfered with the investigation and perhaps destroyed any chance of the
police finding the murderer. In self-defense, I must
keep quiet."

"All right then, keep quiet."

"But I can't sit idly by and let the killer escape.
My self-respect won't allow it."

"Nuts to your self-respect. You're an actor, your
contract says so. It doesn't say anything about being
a detective."

"You may as well save your breath, Melva. I'm in
this, and I'm staying in. How about some food?"

"Do you think you can find out who killed him?"
Fred said.

"I think so. In fact, I'm sure of it."

"Then I'll fix up a series of releases. Police baffled,
but Sanders is working on it and promises developments. We'll keep shooting those in and then really
spread it when you catch the guy."

"You do," Melva said grimly, "and I'll stake you
out on an ant-hill and spread cake icing all over you.

If George must be an idiot, the safest thing he can do is be one secretly. Why give the pot-shotter a motive to ring up a bull's eye on George?"

"I don't want the story in print, anyway," I said.

Fred was incredulous. "You don't *what?* You must want publicity; that's what you hired me for. Why, this thing is a natural. Every editor on the coast would go for it. There's thousands of dollars' worth of publicity in it."

"I'd look a prize fool," I said. "If I had been asked to aid the police, I'd say go ahead. As it is, it would be regarded as a publicity stunt."

"So what?" Fred said. "Since when is publicity bad for an actor?"

"But I'm not doing this for publicity. I'm doing it first because I must, second because I think people who murder other people oughtn't to get away with it. And here's another point: if you announce that I'm working on the case, wouldn't I look silly if I didn't solve it?"

"But you said you could."

"And I think I can. But I'm not Superman. I'm not even the Saint. I'm just Sanders."

"This isn't like you, George," Fred said.

"My gastric juices are aflow," I said. "Let us go. This conversation is futile."

We went to the hotel, so that Fred and Melva could register. The night clerk seemed happy to see smooth faces. "Me and my little grandson started to play 'Beaver' before I come on shift," he said. "Counted so many beards we get hoarse yellin'. Enough stuffing in this town to keep a mattress factory hummin' for a week. You two married?"

"No," Fred said. "Damn it."

"Don't make no difference," the clerk said. "I'll put you in the same room if you want. I always say if people are gonna sleep together, separate rooms won't stop 'em. All it does is give one or t'other a cold, runnin' up and down the halls barefoot. There's nothing vacant but one big room with a double bed, and a little rat nest on the top floor that I charge two dollars for. It's pretty lousy, if you ask me. Too much money, too."

"I'll take the little one," Fred said. "Give her the other."

"Makin' a mistake, young feller." He looked at Melva through, over, and under steel-rimmed spectacles. He spread a snaggled grin. "Big mistake."

"Never mind," Fred said, through clenched teeth.

"No call to get het up," the old man said. "Most natural thing in the world. Fun, too. I ain't forgot. Never will, I reckon. Sign here."

Fred and Melva signed. She took her key and went up to wash her face. We promised to meet her in the bar next door, and started out.

We found almost everybody in the bar. Everybody except Sammy. There were Paul, Riegleman, Curtis, the boss cameraman, and a frieze of bearded extras. I stopped at Riegleman's table.

"Is there a decent eating place around here?" I asked.

"I tried that counter joint down the street," Paul

answered. "I ordered a filet, medium. When I stuck a fork in it, it whinnied. All that steak needed was a good vet, and you could enter it at Santa Anita."

"I say," Riegleman objected, blinking. "You didn't really get horse-meat?"

"Oh no?" Paul said. "Then why did it flinch when I rattled my spurs?"

Riegleman stared for a moment, then his long face relaxed. "I see," he said. "You're having me on."

I thought that now was as good a time as any. "I've taken rather a liberty," I said, "but in a good cause, I trust." I gave Riegleman an apologetic smile. "I've removed the reel of film that was being shot at the time of the murder, and put it in a safe place."

Jaws dropped. Riegleman grew a "how-dare-you" look in his eye. Before he could speak, I said lightly, "Don't worry about the film, it's hidden in my trailer."

"But why?" Paul demanded.

"It points out the murderer," I said. "And my detective training seems to be getting the upper hand. as soon as I get that film into Hollywood and get it developed and a print made, I'll be able to call in the police and say, 'There's the man.'"

"Who do you think did it?" Riegleman asked idly.

"I didn't. And nobody else who was in the scene. It must have been someone behind the cameras. I have it narrowed down to two." I grinned. "You're both alibied, I suppose."

Riegleman looked at me in the same way he had stared at Paul. Presently, he smiled. "You're guying us, George."

"Maybe. There must be something highly significant on that reel. I think it will point out the murderer."

"No kidding?" Paul asked. He frowned. "You'd better not spread the word until you're sure, George. You'll get yourself bumped."

"Where is your bodyguard?" Riegleman demanded. "I issued orders."

"Fred and Melva," I told him. "They just came up. They'll keep me safe from harm. God help anybody who tries to incapacitate me while Melva's around. She'd bite his jugular."

"You must let the police handle this, George," Riegleman said, suddenly grim. "You're too valuable a property. If you have any ideas about the identity of the murderer, tell the sheriff. We cannot allow you to run risks."

"I'm on my way to the sheriff's office now," I lied. "Then I'm going to eat."

Melva came along, was highly cordial to Riegleman, and we went out. We met Sammy coming in.

"I'm sorry, George," he said, "but I had carburetor trouble, and I've been in a garage since I left you. I haven't told anybody."

"I told Riegleman and Paul, Sammy. You get the others. We're going to dinner. Know a good place?"

"Up the coast about ten miles," Sammy said. "Lee's Kitchen. Good food, but too expensive."

"See you later, then."

When we were at Fred's car, I paused, staggered a little, put one hand to my forehead and clutched the car door with the other. Melva was at my side in something less than a second, grabbing my elbow. Her face was the color of the under side of a trout. *"George!"*

"Sorry," I gasped. "I'm desperately tired. Not much sleep last night, and now—all this. And I *must* be made up by eight tomorrow." I leaned against the side of the car and tried to look faint. "If I could only get some sleep!"

She fell for it. "Never mind about dinner, George. We'll take you back to the trailer. I'll make you some soup."

"I had soup," I mumbled. "Just sleep." I half closed my eyes, and Melva and Fred helped me into the car. They helped me out of it when we got to the trailer. I pulled myself together at the trailer door, looked at my watch, and said, "I'll be able to get six hours sleep. Just don't disturb me in the meantime."

"George," Melva said, "about this killing—"

"Tell you tomorrow," I said. "You don't want my work to suffer, do you?"

"Heaven forbid," she said. "George, would you like us to tuck you in?"

"No," I said firmly. *"No!"*

I watched them drive away. Then I went inside, put the searchlight back into the photo-electric circuit, made sure the film can was still there, got my gun, and sat in the dark. Since Sammy hadn't spread the story, it was not yet too late.

Why had Wanda come, then? I had supposed that she had come in response to Sammy's tale. Her implied explanation just didn't make sense. In fact I couldn't see Wanda in this at all. Why was she suddenly out of character? Not the screen character, the demure little thing spreading light among the dark and darkened. But her off-stage character.

I knew Wanda. I knew her as what was known, among actors, cameramen, make-up artists, dress designers, and the rest, as a Good Kid. A girl with a sense of fun, who occasionally thought of weird and hilarious practical jokes. She didn't fit into this new siren role at all.

Because it was definitely a role, and she was proving to be a definitely bad off-stage actress.

Why? Why was she deliberately taking on that role?

What had she been doing in Severance Flynne's room? What was the business of the fingerprints?

Why had she showed up here, slipping through the dark to my door?

I had to shrug off the questions, for I heard somebody else coming through the dark to my door. Somebody else? How did I know? It might be Wanda again. I had a sudden, depressing picture of her constantly arriving, bathed in the brilliance of my searchlight. I sighed and picked up my gun.

The light switched on, and Listless Nelson shielded her eyes with a furred arm. She was dressed for a hard winter in what might have been dyed lemming, and a pair of denim slacks.

I fixed the lights. "Come in," I said wearily. "I don't want to seem inhospitable, but I want to know why you're here, and why you enter uninvited."

She wasn't embarrassed. She wasn't brazen. She was just terribly earnest. "I've got to talk to somebody," she whispered.

"You could go on the radio," I said. "Listen, Miss

Nelson, I warn you that you'll get into serious difficulties if you don't give me some answers. Where were you when Flynne was killed?"

Her eyes widened. "Why, I was watching Sammy telling everybody how to do right." Her eyes became softly blue. "Gee, he's swell."

I looked at a spot just over her head for a moment. If she had been watching Sammy, and if Sammy was behind the cameras, what else did she see? According to such evidence as I had, the shot had come from near—or in line with—the first camera. I tried to put myself in a position that might correspond to hers. There would have been Riegleman, Sammy, the script girl, the cameraman, in one group. Then the boom crew and the technicians scattered around in the foreground. She would have had almost all of the possible suspects in sight.

"Miss Nelson," I said. "How is your memory?"

"I won a prize in reciting, in seventh grade. But I don't think Sammy would be interested."

"I might be," I said. "Try to pretend you're back on the set today when Severance Flynne was shot. Try to remember if you noticed anything that seemed unusual."

She didn't understand. She stared blankly from enormous blue eyes.

I explained. "I'll stake my shirt that nobody in the scene killed him, Miss Nelson. The psychology is all wrong. If I'm correct, then someone behind the camera shot him, and behind the first camera, at that. So we know the approximate location from which the shot was fired. If you were watching Sammy, you had a large group under observation. Did any of that group do anything out of character?"

"I don't know," she said in a small voice. "I didn't pay any attention to anybody but Sammy. That's what I want to talk to you about."

A sudden thought struck me. Maybe Sammy had done something unusual. Perhaps that was what she was trying to tell me.

"Yes," I said softly. "Tell me."

"Well, uh, my mother told me about him when I told her he had come to work on our lot. Mother said she saw him when he was a boy, dancing. And she said he was like a bird. That's what she always said, a bird. Sometimes she said a hummingbird, but mostly just any old bird. And I couldn't see how, Mr. Sanders. He's so fat, and all. But mother talked a lot about him, and I started watching him when I could, and you know he sort of walks graceful. Like he didn't have any body, sort of. And then I accidentally waited for him one night, when I knew he was coming out the gate, and we—well—got acquainted. And, Mr. Sanders, I *like* him. I even told mother, and, well, he came to dinner, and we started seeing previews together, and he bought me a compact once. And now, *this*. It's awful!"

I didn't dare distract her. I sat quietly while she sniffled into a ridiculous piece of chiffon. She raised her eyes, which were beginning to puff under the lids.

"He stood me up!" she wailed. "He was supposed to see me tonight, and it's almost ten o'clock. He's mad because I threw those old guns away, but I did it just to keep him out of trouble. What can I do, Mr. Sanders, what can I do?"

I felt like slapping her. "Did you come over here just for that? Slipping into my trailer when it looked empty? Really?"

"I got so worried," she said tearfully. "I thought he might be here, and when I saw it was dark, I thought he might come back. I was just going to come in out of the cold. I wasn't even going to turn on your lights."

I looked at her until she dropped her eyes. Was she telling the truth? If so, she was a liability here, and the best I could do would be to throw her out. On the other hand, she was quite possibly lying. This ingenuousness could be a pose. In that case, what could I do? I could accuse her of trying to get the film and destroy it; I could charge her with having fired the fatal shot over the heads of Sammy and the others; I could demand a reason why she had tried to incriminate and then to kill me—

But could I? Had she had an opportunity to switch guns on me? I couldn't remember. She could have been in that group around me when the scene ended, and have escaped notice. For, although she was pretty, she was colorless. I wouldn't have seen her if she hadn't wanted me to see her. No, all I could do was accept her story and give fatherly advice.

"The moon won't sulk," I said, "if you don't see Sammy tonight. It'll be around tomorrow night, and fuller, too. As a matter of fact, Sammy has been working with me tonight. He couldn't get away. But he should be almost finished by now. He may be waiting at your place."

"Oh, heavens!" she cried. "And if I'm not there, he won't wait."

She turned and ran. I sighed and began fussing with the searchlight again, and she stuck her head back in the door.

"Gee, thanks, Mr. Sanders!" she said. She pulled her head out of the door like a blonde cork, and padded off across the sand.

Had the trap been sprung? I pondered on this as I sat in the dark. Oh, the trap had been sprung in the physical sense. Twice. Wanda and Listless. Melva, too, for that matter. But had I baited the trap for a weasel and caught three mice?

Wanda was off the list of suspects. But was it possible that she had seen the killer and was afraid to tell? She knew Flynne, slightly at least. Could she have known the motive? Was that why she went to his room? To collect evidence, or destroy it? Was she hiding the killer?

Had Listless killed him? Was she capable of even firing a gun, much less performing a feat of marksmanship that would spin William Cody in his grave?

I had a bookful of questions, but not a word of answers. And, besides, I was beginning to get sleepy. My mental stature didn't come in for many kudos there in the dark, empty trailer.

My next visitor was Riegleman.

Chapter Eleven

"TURN THAT BLOODY THING OFF!" he yelled, as the beam blinded him. "Are you trying to sear my eyeballs?"

I did nothing of the sort. I suddenly felt as if my heart had been packed in shaved ice. This was the first time I had ever faced a murderer, and it wasn't like in the movies at all. On the screen I was even a little reckless, daring the murderer to make a move, knowing that I had three tricks—and a knife—up my sleeve. Not here. I didn't want Riegleman even to wiggle his ears.

"What do you want?" I asked, surprised that my voice didn't squeak.

"I want to talk to you. What the hell did you think?" he shouted. "Put out that blasted light!"

The ice melted around my heart, and I did things about lights. I held the gun in my jacket pocket, though, with a sweaty hand.

"People don't usually come slipping into dark houses," I pointed out, "to talk to absent occupants. You knew I was intending to eat dinner."

"I owe you an apology, of course," he admitted.

"May I sit down, or does that gun mean that I must elevate my hands?"

I took my hand, empty, out of my pocket. "I'm a little quick," I said. "Did you kill Severance Flynne?"

He stared at me, as if I were something out of Lewis Carroll. A slithy tove, for example.

"I just wanted to know," I told him. "You see, I have contrived a ruse to trap a murderer. You knew about it, for I told you myself. When I saw you come in that door, I felt that you could be after only one thing—proof of guilt. Although," I added wryly, "I must admit that door has been busy as the entrance to a pub on a hot day. Well, what did you want to talk about?"

Riegleman's gloomy eyes were accusing. "I went to see the sheriff. You told me you were on your way there. You didn't go. I want to know why. I ordered you to drop all this nonsense about catching a murderer. We're up here to shoot a picture, not to let you lose sleep. Nor to let you be killed. You're a valuable property."

"Do you realize," I said, "that a human being has been murdered, and that the value of a human life is far above any shadow play you may produce?"

He stared at me. "Neither of us ever heard of this, uh, Flynne, is it? I, for one, don't know any more about him than I did before he was killed. Oh, I'm sorry for the poor fellow. But his death means very little more to me than the death of a native in the Australian bush. But, this project means a great deal to me. *Seven Dreams* is very likely to be my triumph. Yours, too, George, if you pay attention to business."

"Let me clarify my place in this situation, Riegleman. I am in a position to learn who killed a man. Peculiar circumstances have put me in that position. I must do what I can—for reasons which we won't go into here."

"Why not? Let's go into them. I'm interested."

"No." Could I tell him that I had had the murder gun in my possession, that I had lied to the police, that I had withheld evidence, that Lamar James might come looking for me at any moment? I could imagine his screams of rage. Riegleman would fight for his budget like a tiger for her cub.

"Very well," he said calmly. "You say that you must persist in this idiotic conduct, I say that you must not. We reach an impasse, then. I should imagine that your contract has a clause covering such a condition. We can invite you to give up your professional career and starve as a private detective.

"George," he went on in exasperation, "you won't make a farthing even if you succeed in this folly. That's what I can't comprehend. There's nothing in it for you."

There was deep feeling in this. I knew that Riegleman's attitude toward money was intense, and of long standing. Which gave me a lever.

"I suppose," I said, lightly, "that you could dismiss me if I jeopardized the picture against orders. On the other hand, I feel certain that you wouldn't like to see me go."

"Of course I wouldn't like it, George, old boy. I think you're magnificent in the role!"

"Thanks. Neither would you like the expensive delay entailed in replacing me. Eh?"

"Quite right."

"That puts me in a position to make a trade, then. I promise you that I won't jeopardize the picture. If I fail at any time to give a performance that is unaffected by my activity in this matter, I will give up my investigations without a mutter. How say you, sir?"

"A fair compromise, George. Shall we let it stand at that. Righto?"

"Righto."

We parted friends once more. But when I turned off the light again, I puzzled over Riegleman. Had he told the truth? It was likely that his first consideration would be the picture. On the other hand, had he come to wait in the dark for me, to kill me when I came in?

More questions. No answers.

I couldn't fit any of the persons who had been apparently caught in my trap into the role of murderer. Listless had the opportunity, perhaps, but she was miscast as a killer. Wanda hadn't known it was a trap. Melva was an almost impossible choice, and Riegleman, if he hadn't lied about not knowing Flynne, had no motive.

One fact became clear to me: the motive had to be strong. The murderer *had* to be a person with initiative, cunning, and an amazing ability to shoot straight. Given that type in the circumstances that obtained out there in the sand, still you must admit that he ran many chances of failure. He must be certain to kill with one shot, from a considerable distance, a man who was supposed to be jumping around as if redskins were about to drill him with an arrow. He must time his shot so that it was obscured by other noises. He must be able to get rid of the weapon. He must be above public suspicion. The motive, to match these specifications, must have been—!

I began to feel sorry for the person hag-ridden by something which could force him to such lengths. Granting him all the necessary attributes, still he must have known the risks. If his need to kill Flynne outweighed his chance of failure, that need must have indeed been great.

Then I thought of his attempt to kill me, and my sympathy for him did a power dive.

At about that time, I heard my door begin to open again, slowly, cautiously. But this time when the light flashed on there was no shaved ice around my heart. I was becoming inured to facing murderers. I was not even amazed at my steady voice when I said to Paul:

"I have you covered."

"Then you don't need that beacon," he replied. "What is this, a police line-up?"

"Breaking and entering might lead to one."

"Who's breaking and entering?" he demanded. "I came over here to wait for you to come back from dinner. I want to talk to you."

"One would think I was the producer on this job," I said, "the way people seek me out. There, is that light better? Now. Did you kill Severance Flynne?"

"Oh, sure," he jeered. "I wanted to save the company a lunch. You know how prices are these days."

His black eyes were candid, even a trifle insolent. I said, "Sit down, Paul. You wanted to talk to me?"

"Yeah," he said. "I just had a thought. It's funny, when you come to think of it, that the only guy who wasn't hired on this picture, the only guy who had a phony work slip, was killed. I don't know what it means, but it's funny, and I thought I'd mention it. Good night."

"One moment. It seems strange that you would come all the way out here from town, and then slip into a dark trailer only for that. You could have told me tomorrow."

"Sure. But I didn't want to tell you tomorrow. I wanted to tell you tonight. And I didn't know your trailer was dark till I was within ten feet of it. Your shades might have been drawn. But I did know that you'd be along. So I thought I'd wait here. If the door wasn't open, I was going to sit on the step. In any case, I wasn't going to walk out to my car and get my shoes full of sand again."

"But why tell me? Why not tell the sheriff?"

"Hell, you're the great detective. I wanted to see if you'd thought of that angle."

"I hadn't, if it makes you feel any better."

"It does. So long." He vanished into the darkness.

Even before I could rearrange the lights, I had another visitor. This was Curtis, the head cameraman, who gave me the impression he was walking around six inches below sea level. He almost had to lean backward to look me in the eye.

"I saw your light, he said apologetically. "I hope I'm not intruding."

"You're the first person who has given the matter a thought, Mr. Curtis. Come in, by all means."

"I came about the film," he said.

I offered him a cigarette. "I'd like to keep it a while longer," I said. "If you can possibly do without it."

"It would be all right with me, Mr. Sanders. But you know Mr. Riegleman. We'd all lose our jobs."

"Don't worry," I said. "He was here only a few minutes ago. He knows I have it. He said nothing."

Curtis looked uncomfortable and unhappy. "I know that. But it's got to be expressed to the studio by midnight with the rest of the film. You know how Mr. Riegleman is."

I did know. I said, "If I bring it over before then, will it be all right?"

"Well," Curtis said, "I guess so. But it would be damned embarrassing for us if you didn't. If anything should happen, I mean. You'd have to cover up for us."

"I will, if it's necessary."

He thanked me, grinned, and went away.

I went back to my vigil, which was beginning to seem useless. It was unreasonable to suppose that the murderer, if he hadn't already been here, wouldn't have seen my lights blinking on and off like battleship signals. And if he had intended to steal the film, he'd have given up by now. It would be like trying to steal a pet elephant from a Republican convention.

I ran over the list. All of the principal suspects had

wandered in during the evening, except Carla and Sammy. Listless, Riegleman, Paul, and, yes, Curtis. He didn't look or act like a killer, but, being the boss cameraman, he would be able to wander about without arousing suspicion. Since his work was done *before* the cameras began to roll—in lining up the scenes—he could have found time to aim a gun.

I considered the point raised by Paul. It did seem odd that Flynne, out of three hundred accredited persons, should have been in the way of that one shot. The fact admitted several interpretations, however. The death of Flynne, as such, could have been an accident. The murderer could have aimed at someone else and missed. Not daring to risk another shot, he could have got rid of the gun. In that case, he was biding his time, and we would have another killing.

Another possibility was that the killer had arranged for Flynne to get his spurious work slip so that he would remain anonymous for a time after the killing, which time the killer would use either in escaping or covering up. I didn't like this idea. If the shot had come from behind the camera, the killer was not an extra. He could, therefore, manage to get Flynne a bona fide job in time.

These thoughts and their variations began to rattle around in my head, and I dozed off.

The lights brought me awake, blinking in unison with my caller. Covering a yawn, I said, "This is a pleasure, Carla. I feared you were ignoring me."

Chapter Twelve

SHE LOOKED AT ME, and for the fourth time said, "But I can't tell you, I just can't!"

We had had nearly an hour of this, and I had seen her become a frightened child. She was not Carla, the dark lady of mystery in *Salted Wine;* she was not the reckless wench of *Calcutta Callie;* nor a Barbary babe. She was a simple youngster with fear in her heart.

"If you won't tell me," I said, "I can't know what I'm protecting you *from.* Do you want me to guess?"

She looked down at her trim feet. "What would you guess?" she whispered.

"I'd guess that you had something to do with Flynne's death. Shall I go further?"

Her head jerked up in a marionette motion. "I didn't! I wouldn't! The last thing I ever wished him was harm!"

"What kind of a guy was he?" I asked quietly.

It caught her off guard. "He was sweet," she said reminiscently. "He was sweet and full of dreams. He wanted to be a great engineer once. Then he wanted to be a great pilot. After that, a great financier, a star salesman, and last, a great actor. He was never a great anything."

She realized that she had told me that she had known him well. Her dark eyes had something of defiance, and something of dislike in them. "You tricked me," she said.

"Since you told me this much, you may as well tell me the rest."

"Let me tell you how it is with me," she said slowly, and little bitter memories were in her voice. "I was a kid from Brooklyn, P.S. one-sixty-four. I was clerking in a dime store, and one day, when I was window-wishing on my lunch hour, Gary Blake came up and asked me if I wanted to go to Hollywood. I told him I'd call a cop and all three of us would talk it over, and he said swell. He called the cop. He really was a talent scout. A ham hawk, he said. He gave me some money and a ticket on a plane, and I didn't even go home to mend the run in my best pair of stockings. That dime store still owes me a week's wages."

She grinned wryly, and for a moment the fear had gone.

"That's how sick I was of everything," she said. "So I got here in a bargain basement dress, no stockings, and a new name."

"What was your real name?"

"That doesn't matter," she said. "I worked hard, George, I really did. I had to learn to speak English correctly. I had to learn to walk. I had to change my hands from stalks of limp bananas to useful objects. I found out that you could go hungry for three days

and not die, and I know what it is to snag a stock-
ing on the way to a screen test. Those are the things I
learned. What I had, I kept—slim hips, full breasts,
and a good face. I was built and looked like a siren.
I had to learn to act one. But I did, George, and it's
the thing I'm most proud of. And I can't stand to
have it taken away from me. I can't! That's why I
want you to help me."

"Who would try to take it from you?"

"Everybody, if I'm connected with poor Sev's killing. That deputy sheriff this morning practically
accused me of shooting him. I know he could see how
frightened I was. I was terrified, and from his viewpoint there wasn't any reason for it if I was innocent.
But I am, George, I swear it, and I want you to keep
anybody from asking me questions. Because I don't
trust myself. I'll go to pieces!"

"I don't like it," I said. "You're asking me to take
you on trust, and although I'm inclined to do it,
I can't unless you do the same for me. I love beautiful women, baby. I think they're Nature's noblest.
Every time I see one, I want to battle a windmill.
But this is such a serious situation that I don't dare,
unless you tell me what it's all about. I give you my
word of honor that I won't let out your secret."

She stared miserably at the floor, a slump in those
lovely shoulders. Her polo coat hung slackly, and her
fingers fiddled aimlessly with each other. She was
looking at pictures. I could see them trooping out of
the past, a parade of formless forms behind the dark
veil of her eyes.

I wanted a cigarette. I wanted a drink, and I was

hungry as a flame. I dared not move. I even tried to hold my corpuscles still. Maybe she'd tell, and we could wind this up in a few moments.

I felt that I had all the information that was necessary to point out the killer. Somewhere along the line of suspects who had visited me this evening, I had learned a disturbing fact. What it was I didn't know, but it began to disturb me as I waited for Carla to make up her mind. Was it a word, a gesture, a start, an expression of attitude, a question? I needed a cue to the clue. Perhaps Carla could give it.

I reflected that I could be overwrought and romanticizing, but still it stood to reason that if the killer was among my visitors, then he had come to see what I knew. He must have betrayed his purpose, and I must have observed that betrayal. Perhaps I had buried the observation deep in my subconscious for reasons of psychological distaste. I needed a spur to force it out in the open.

Carla knew something important. That was obvious.

"George." Her voice was a hoarse whisper. Not deliberately hoarse, not deliberately a whisper. She wasn't acting, not now. What she had to tell was something she couldn't say out loud. "It was years ago. Why can't it be forgotten?"

"A man is dead," I reminded her. "One Severance Flynne. And you knew him well enough to refer to him as *Sev*." In a spot like this, I remembered, *The Falcon* tapped a cigarette against his thumbnail. I tried it. It was an old cigarette, and half the tobacco spilled out. I threw it away.

"Why shouldn't I call him Sev?" she demanded, almost defensively. "He was—"

A foot crunched in the gravel outside the trailer. Carla's voice stopped as though someone had lifted a needle off a record. There was a soft, gentle tap on the door.

I thought "Damn!" and said, "Come in."

A beard came in through the door.

You get to think of them as beards. They seem to think of themselves as beards. Someone puts up a sign in the casting office, "Beards this way," and everybody with more than half an inch of fuzz on his face moves in that direction. They take on a curious anonymity. Beards, brown. Beards, white. Beards, long. Beards, trimmed.

Severance Flynne had been a beard.

So was this guy who'd tapped lightly at my trailer door. It took me a good five seconds to recognize him.

"Mr. Sanders," he said apologetically. "I'm sorry to disturb you. But you *are* the star of this picture, aren't you?"

"So my agent tells me," I said. I was still cross at the interruption.

"Then. Then perhaps. Perhaps *you* can tell me what I'm supposed to do."

The bewildered look in his eyes would have made nicks in a heart of stone.

"See here," I said. "Haven't you been in pictures before?"

He shook his head. "No. And it's very confusing. You see, I don't know just what I'm supposed to be doing here—"

I confess that I drew a long breath, squared off, and prepared to deliver a lecture. Luckily that was the moment when Sammy came in.

He stared around the trailer, focused on the beard, and said, "Oh, it's you again."

"I'm sorry to have disturbed Mr. Sanders," the beard said unhappily, "but it's just that I don't quite know what I'm supposed to do."

"Just watch the director," Sammy said.

"Oh," the beard said. He paused. "Oh. Thanks." He walked to the trailer door and paused again. "Only you see. My agent said—"

"Never pay any attention to what an agent says," Sammy said in his friendliest tone. "You just turn in your slips and collect your pay and everything will be swell, see?"

The beard looked as bewildered as ever, but he said 'Thanks' all over again before he went out the door and disappeared into the night like a drop of water disappearing down a drain.

"And now," Sammy began.

Carla rose.

All the fright was gone. She was once more in character, smooth, suave, perfectly poised. "Hello, Sammy," she said. She turned to me. "Thanks so much, George," she said warmly. "We'll see how the scene plays tomorrow."

Sammy looked after her for a moment. "Well," he said, "did the trap work?"

"This trailer," I said wryly, "had all the aspects of a drug store telephone booth this evening. Everybody came, for one good-sounding reason or another."

I told him in detail. He shook his head. "I can't make anything of it. Well, I'd better return that film."

"I'll take it back," I said firmly. "You go see List-less. I can see her hunched in misery over a pound of chocolates, listening for your step."

Sammy grinned. "Well, thanks. Keep 'em crying isn't exactly my motto, but a little of it helps."

He left, walking, as I noticed, with an airy grace. I cut all the lights but one and sat in the dimness, thinking.

I wasted no time on guessing at Carla's relationship to Flynne. I tried to deduce from her attitude the fact or facts that would help tag the killer. I was convinced again that I had all the facts necessary to point out the killer, and deduction alone could do it.

But I was tired, and my thought processes wandered into odd channels. Presently I found myself concentrated on my own telephone problem.

One of the necessary evils of our civilization is that instrument invented by Don Ameche and Alexander Bell. You may be in the middle of your bath, but if the phone rings you draggle out to answer it, spotting rugs and, likely as not, answering the doorbell too. You can be jerked out of a sound sleep at three a.m. to fumble in the dark and tell some halfwit that this is not the Superba Doughnut Company; and not be able to sleep again for wondering what kind of hours they work at Superba. You cannot imagine any privacy which the telephone bell cannot invade.

I have had my share of such invasions, and I had

been working on a solution for several months before the *Seven Dreams* episode. I had installed a loudspeaker and microphone in each room of my Hollywood apartment, connected respectively to the receiver and transmitter of my phone, through an amplifier. When my phone rang, a relay was set in motion that, in effect, lifted the receiver. If I were in, say, my big chair, reading a script, all I needed to do was answer in a clear voice. The microphone in my living room ran it through the amplifier to the telephone to the caller. When the caller answered, his voice came through the loudspeakers located all over the place. So, I did no dripping from bathrooms or wandering in cold darkness.

But I couldn't hang up.

I had been unable to devise a means of breaking the connection automatically. Until it was broken, nobody could call me. I thought about this, seeing in my mind's eye the various circuits affected, trying to fasten on the answer.

I hadn't realized that I was tired until electrical circuits, murderers, guns, clues, and a few stray gremlins began to do an insane ballet dance against the darkness in the trailer. Then I closed my eyes. Tomorrow would just have to be another day, whether it wanted to or not.

It wasn't a sound that woke me, some time later, it was a presence. Someone was in the trailer, someone moving so quietly that there wasn't the faintest shadow of a sound. I lay still for a minute or two, my eyes closed, pretending sleep. But whoever was in the trailer had already looked to make sure I wasn't awake, and wasn't paying any attention to me. I lifted my eyelids a fraction of an inch. Then I sat up, wide awake now.

"Hey," I said angrily. "What are you doing in here at this time of night?"

Wanda Waite stared at me and turned white. She was dressed in stout walking shoes, a sheer nightgown, and a massive fur coat. She looked very beautiful, and very worried.

"George—I came in to talk to you, and you were asleep. So I decided not to bother you."

"The way people wander through here, you'd think it was a public lavatory. Well, I'm awake now. What do you want?"

"It can wait until morning," she said. "Sorry."

"I'll drag you back by the hair," I threatened, and I think I meant it. "You'd better whip up an explanation. Twice tonight you've sneaked in here. Now, my heart is all for lady burglars. I think it's a wide open field for females. But when I'm affected, I want to know why. *Why?*"

"It wasn't important," she said nervously. "I said I was sorry I bothered you. Good night."

A new voice came out of the darkness outside. "Do you live here?" Lamar James asked, coming to the door.

Wanda went into her act again. "Please, Mr. James, this was our secret. Don't give it away."

"What secret?" I demanded.

"Thank you, George," she murmured huskily. "You don't need to protect me. I'm not ashamed of it, and besides, Mr. James won't tell. Will you, Mr. James?"

James looked at her for a moment, his eyes an imponderable black in the dim light. "You're under arrest," he said formally. "It is my duty to warn you that anything you say may be used against you."

This was different. "What's the charge?" I demanded. "She didn't kill Flynne, and I can prove it."

"You'll have your chance," James said. "I tried to get her to cooperate, but all she did was act mysterious. She isn't to be charged—yet. She's to be held for questioning in connection with the killing of Severance Flynne. Her fingerprints were all over his room, and I want to know why."

This stopped me. I tried to remember what I had seen of her actions through the crack in Flynne's closet door. Hadn't she had sense enough to wear gloves, or wipe off fingerprints? I couldn't remember her doing either.

Wanda didn't seem perturbed. She glanced down at her costume. "May I go to my room and change? You don't want to take me to jail in my nightgown, do you?"

James said, "All right. Come on."

"I'll get you out, Wanda," I said. "They can't do this to you."

"Thank you, George," she said. "I knew that you, if no one else, would stick by me. Everything has been wonderful, dear, and I hope you sleep well. Dream of me—a little."

When you run up against something unexplainable, you give up trying. I sat there in a numb state until I thought of the time. I looked at my watch and leaped up. I had about ten minutes to return the film, under the deadline.

I looked in the window seat that opens into a bed when you press the right button. The reel of film I'd counted on to prove my innocence was gone.

I had a sudden, uneasy feeling that it had left the trailer under Wanda's fur coat.

Chapter Thirteen

At the crack of 7:30 the next morning, J. Brewster Wallingford came sorrowfully into my trailer. I was folding the electric grill back into its daytime role of writing desk. The little man fixed great brown eyes on me and shook his head.

"It ain't enough," he said sorrowfully, "to get a poor extra killed and pay off his relatives. We got to lose a scene. Plenty I'll give for a story to tell the bank yet. Tell me you got a lead on that can of film, George, tell me."

"I'm sorry, Wally," I said. "I looked where I thought it had to be, and it wasn't."

I thought of my search of Wanda's room. I'd done everything but take off the wallpaper. The can of film wasn't there.

Wallingford dry-washed his hands. "Me, I pick my name for luck," he said. "Brewster for *Brewster's Millions*, and Wallingford for *Get-Rich-Quick*. And what happens? A scene gone, a coming star in jail, and a dead man on the sand. And besides, we lost the author. You can't lose an author, but we did, and he's got to do us a scene with desert sunset. Is this luck? I'm asking."

"You're not obligated to pay Flynne's relatives," I said. "You're not to blame."

"Did you ever lose a son, George?" he asked. "No, you didn't. There ain't anything so bad. I just got to give his family something. They can take a trip, or buy a house. It don't bring back the son, but it takes their mind off."

"You're a good chap, Wally," I said.

"George," he said gloomily, "you shouldn't ought to have taken that film. Honest, you shouldn't."

"What do you want to do about it?"

"What can I do?" he asked. "Can I say 'good-by, George, we don't want you no more'? We got money invested in you. And I can't make you pay for retaking the scene. You thought what you did was right. Everybody guesses wrong sometimes. I got to take it, that's all. But you made a deal with Riegleman, so you got to drop whatever you're doing about this murder."

He had me there. Certainly the loss of that can of film had jeopardized the picture. I'd have to stick to my word. What, then, of those two guns on the sand dune? What of my fingerprints on the gun found in Carla's wagon? What of my lie about having carried .45's?

We couldn't shoot the scene over with me carrying .45's, for in the earlier sequence I had been shown clearly with pearl-handled guns. It wouldn't matter to James what I carried in the retake, but it would to the script girl. Peggy Whittier never missed a trick. She would point out the oversight, and everybody would remember that the gun found in Carla's wagon had a pearl handle. This would bring James and his questions into the picture.

It was open and shut. I *couldn't* give up the investigation. On the other hand, I couldn't go on with it. I'd be fired off the one job that meant more than any other to me. After having had a taste of playing Hilary Weston, I couldn't imagine not being allowed to finish the picture.

As I had told Melva, I'd have played the role for nothing. After too many years of outwitting dull police and distasteful gangsters, I had found a part greatly to be desired. I was given a choice: actor or detective. And I couldn't take one in preference to the other. I *must* be both.

"All right, Wally," I said. "I made my agreement. I'll stick to it."

He took me at my word. His round glowing face showed it. That was the nicest thing about him. He'd believe any lie, even mine.

"George," he said warmly, "sometimes I think you ain't half so bad as people make out. Now we got to get started."

A knock on the door caused me to reflect that somebody was being amazingly polite. I opened it to a telegraph messenger.

"Why don't you sell the goats and move into town," he said, grinning. "I had hell's own time finding you."

"A half dollar's worth?" I asked, reaching in my pocket.

"Thirty-five cents'll cover it," he said. "It wasn't really so tough."

He gave me fifteen cents change and a telegram. It read:

"CAN YOU VERIFY WANDA WAITE AR-RESTED IMMORAL CONDUCT IN MALE ACTOR'S ROOM? TELEPHONE REVERSE CHARGES."

It was signed "Smith." If the situation had been otherwise, I would have grinned. "Smith" was the city editor of a Los Angeles newspaper, and his name wasn't Smith any more than Wally's was Wallingford. He happened to be a friend of mine, and I could detect his wry humor in the wording of the telegram. Only, it wasn't funny. Not this time.

Someone had tipped off the papers that Wanda Waite had been arrested.

I folded the telegram and slipped it in my pocket. "My aunt Maggie got along fine in her tonsillectomy," I said. Then I added, "What are we going to do if someone tips off the papers about Wanda's being arrested?"

Wally moaned softly. "Serpents' teeth we have to have yet. No gratitude, that's what somebody's got. I give 'em jobs, I pay 'em regular, and they stick a lie through my heart for a headline. Who'd tip off the papers?"

I shrugged my shoulders. "Wanda might know. Can we visit her in jail, do you suppose?"

"She ain't in jail," he said. "Not since one o'clock this morning. I told that sheriff I would see personally to his losing the next election, so he turned her out and offered me a drink."

"Let's go see Wanda, then."

On the way to the hotel I asked, "I understand the Brewster and the Wallingford, Wally, but what does the "J" stand for?"

"J. P. Morgan. Why should I be a piker?"

"Oh," I said. I decided not to ask questions. Wallingford, for *Get-Rich-Quick* Wallingford. Brewster, for *Brewster's Millions*. J., for J. P. Morgan.

"Funny," he said, as I parked the car and we started for the lobby, "I never thought much about the J. Now, you got me worrying about it. Now, I got to find out."

"Forget it," I said. "I'll just call you Jackson."

He gave me a worried look and let it go at that.

The same clerk was at the desk. "Don't you ever sleep?" I asked. "Is Miss Waite in?"

He yawned, looked at the register, and gave a low whistle. "Oh, *that* one!" He glanced at the key rack. "Sure is."

"Will you inform her," I said, "that Mr. Sanders and Mr. Wallingford would like to see her?"

He leered. "Why'nt you just walk in on her? I would."

"I think you'd better call her."

"Sissy!" he muttered, and plugged in on the switchboard. "Two gents here to see you," he said. "You want 'em one at a time or all together?" He discon·

nected and did better than Barbara Stanwyck on a "Ch-ch!" "Both of you," he said, winking. "What'll they think of next?"

Wanda's face was scrubbed and shiny. She was in a loose, demure housecoat. Her hair fell in loose golden waves to her shoulders. She looked like a missionary's bride.

"Hello," she said, like a little girl.

"You look sweet," Wallingford said. "Tell me, what's giving?"

"Why, Wally," she said, big-eyed. "I don't know what you mean."

"All these fumadiddles," he said sorrowfully. "You should ought to be ashamed, a nice girl. Going to George's trailer in a nightgown."

"But I wanted to talk to him," she said plaintively. "And a girl would certainly be safe with George. He's so sweet."

Now what was she up to, I wondered. Aside from the veiled insult, she had switched her act completely around. Now she was that fresh young thing known to millions, not the flaming temptress of the night before.

"And now this," I said, giving her the telegram.

She read it. Her lips began to tremble. Her blue eyes glistened with imminent tears. "Who would *do* such a thing?" she pleaded. "I've never harmed anyone. I *like* people. But after all," she went on matter-of-factly, "it's true. All except the immoral conduct. I—" she spread her hands. "I don't know what to say. It's too late to stop the story now, isn't it?"

"Too late to stop what story?" Wally said. He gave me a dirty look, snatched the telegram out of Wanda's hand, glanced at it, and turned gray-white.

"I can still stop it. Only, who sent in the story?" He stared at me accusingly.

"Believe me," I said, putting my heart into it, "I didn't."

"Well, I'll stop it; I'll call up Smith. Smith. Who's this Smith? I'll call the owner of the paper. I'll call my business office, maybe he owes me money. I'll stop the story."

"Can you?" Wanda said, in a little-girl voice. "Gee!"

"Only," Wally said, "who sent it in? You got any ideas?"

She spread her hands helplessly. "Somebody doesn't like me, I guess." Tears began to roll down her pale cheeks.

"Don't talk like that," Wally said comfortingly. "Everybody loves you."

I watched Wanda closely. I felt that she was overacting again. Her timing was still off, she used italics. And a speculative gleam entered her eyes when Wallingford said he could stop the story. None of it made sense.

We left, no wiser than before, and found a public phone in the lobby. While Wallingford called, I loafed outside the booth. Paul and Carla went along the walk outside, deep in conversation. I hadn't known they knew each other. I filed that away for future, if any, use.

A little boy came up to me. He was about eight, and freckled. "Hello, you ham," he said. He turned and ran to the desk.

"Tommy," the old clerk said to him, "Grandpa'll just beat the living hell out of you if you don't stop saying things like that. He's got to make a living some way, ain't he?" He called over to me. " 'Scuse him, Mr. Sanders."

Sammy came in from the elevator.

"Hi, Fat," the little boy said.

Sammy ignored him. "I told you I'd catch hell, George. Riegleman is steaming."

"He is? I thought he never lost his temper."

"He's really steaming," Sammy said. "Just wait till he sees you."

"Hi, Fat," Tommy said.

"Of course," I said, "I'm devilish sorry. But there isn't anything I can do about it. I may be able to find the film. In fact, I think I can promise it."

"You were going to trap a murderer last night, too, George."

"I did."

"Who?" Sammy snapped.

"I don't know, Sammy. But I mean to know. I'll stake my life on the fact that the killer was among my visitors. It remains only to think it through correctly and I'll have him."

"Hi, Fat," Tommy said.

Sammy peered into the phone booth. "What's Mr. Big doing?"

"Squelching, he hopes, a story about Wanda's arrest."

"My God, did somebody give it to the papers?"

"Let's forget it for a moment. Listen, Sammy, we've got to figure out something on those guns. If we retake that scene today, I'll be sunk."

"Me too," Sammy said gloomily. "McGuire asked about 'em again last night. I'll have Listless go out and look for 'em today. That's all I can do. God knows how we'll get that other gun back from James. I guess we really got ourselves into something, George."

"It's beginning to seem so, Sammy."

Wallingford stuck his head out. "He wants to talk to you, George." He followed his head out. "I told him it was a lie, and threatened to take away our advertising, but he says I wasn't here, so how could I tell."

I took up the phone. "Sanders here."

"This is Carl Miller of the *Morning Star*, Mr. Sanders. We met once at an inventors' banquet." I recognized "Smith's" voice.

"I remember very well, Mr. Miller," I said cautiously.

"About this story," he said. "We got it pretty straight. I'd like a confirmation or denial from somebody who was on the scene."

The telephone booth was hot, and filled with the faint fragrance of Wallingford's after-shave lotion.

"The story is untrue," I said. "What do you mean by *pretty* straight?"

"What do *you* mean by untrue?"

"She was in my trailer last night in lounging costume, a big fur coat, and stout walking shoes. She didn't remove so much as a piece of lint from her person. The deputy sheriff came in when she was leaving. He had some questions to ask. They left together."

That was the literal truth.

"I see," he said. "I won't use the story, then. By the way, good luck. I'd like to have a break on the yarn when you catch the guy."

"Uh—what—was—that?"

"Fred Forbes wired me, and I presume the other editors, that you were working on the Flynne killing. Our readers will be agog over that. Nearly everybody thinks of you as a detective."

"I say," I said, "be a good chap and don't print it, will you?"

"I already have," he said. "In three editions."

"Oh, God! Well, I suppose nothing can be done. I'll strike a bargain with you then. If you will tell all the other papers there is nothing in this Wanda Waite story, I'll try to see that you receive special consideration on mine."

"It's a deal. Thanks."

I boiled out of the booth, mayhem in each hand for Fred.

"What gives?" Wallingford asked.

"Murder, maybe. Have either of you seen Fred?"

"The story," Wallingford insisted. "Did you kill it?"

"Oh, that. Yes. It won't run." I paused. "I've got to find Fred. You two go on, I'll be along." I went over to the desk. "Is Mr. Forbes in his room, Uncle?"

He glanced at the register. "Nope. Checked out. Said he was goin' back to Hollywood, th' dope. I wouldn't go off and leave that red-head in a public library, even."

I joined Wallingford and Sammy on their way out. I had agreed not to work on this case any longer, but knew that I could on the quiet. And Fred had spread it over the papers. I didn't like the situation.

I knew that, given a little time, I could find the murderer. And if I did, I'd lose the job I cared most to hold.

"Damn," I said, as we went through the door.

"Good-by, Fat," Tommy called after us.

Chapter Fourteen

RIEGLEMAN WAS FURIOUS, but Wallingford could heave his weight about with anybody. They made a curious single impression as they glared at each other in the huge trailer that served as the company office. Each was a quiet man, with a calm exterior. Each imparted a sense of great power on the leash.

Neither raised his voice. They might have been discussing the third at Pimlico. But Riegleman's eyes were black with fury, and his long brown hands were tense on his desk. Wallingford's brown eyes had snapping little lights in them, and his pudgy hands, clasped across his paunch, showed white at the knuckles.

"If the film turns up," Riegleman said quietly, "then we've wasted time and money in shooting the scene again. And we can't hope to duplicate that splendid performance of yesterday."

"You speak true," Wallingford murmured sadly. "You can't kill a man but once. But if the film don't walk up and say *Papa*, we're fish in a kettle. We can't take a chance on the weather. Was this really desert, we could count on plenty of sun. But you can almost throw a rock in the ocean from here. We'll shoot it over.

This made sense, and Riegleman's attitude was puzzling. True, he watched his budget like a father watching a virgin daughter. On the other hand, he wasn't a person to take risks. If the film turned up, we could use the better of the two, but we must be certain of one. His anger, though controlled, showed him dead set against retaking the scene.

I put in my oar, and Sammy and Paul looked at me slaunchwise. Their eyes told me how many kinds of a fool I was to get into this fight.

"I feel certain that I can locate the film, Wally," I said. "I can't guarantee it, but I think I know where it went."

"George, you're a good boy," Wallingford said. "And I like you a lot, *but*. Why didn't you get it already? And where is the killer you thought you could catch?"

"I was theoretically correct," I said.

"Sure, sure," he soothed. "You're smart, too. But you didn't deliver nothing, George, but a hole in the budget. You play detectives good, my boy, when somebody writes the dialogue. But this ain't play. We got to take that scene over. Besides, we can't shoot the sunset till the author writes one. And where is he? The office says he's here, but I never seen an author yet that wouldn't let you know. So we shoot the scene over. And that's my final word."

Wallingford went out. Riegleman looked at Sammy.

"All right," he said with a set face. "Let's get at it."

Sammy came to my dressing room as I finished making up. He carried two holstered .45 Colt revolvers on a cartridge belt gleaming with brass shells.

"Listless couldn't find the guns," he said gloomily. "And I can't stall McGuire much longer."

I buckled on the belt. "We can't possibly get away with this, Sammy. Peggy has an eagle eye. She'll spot the change of guns, McGuire will be called into it, and that peering sound will be you and me from behind the eight ball."

"What do you want to do, then? Throw in your hand?"

"I can't. James would arrest me sure as hell. He would have last night, if Wanda hadn't made a diversion. All I can see to do is go out there and hope."

"That hope's as slim as I used to be. But I'll tell you what, I'll try to keep Peggy interested in something else. If I can keep her eye off you, maybe we can get away with it."

I thought of my past life as I went out to get my horse, and speculated on the changes that might be wrought here this morning. Until now it had been a good life: Manchester Technical School, cotton brokerage, four years in Patagonia with a tobacco firm, and finally into this ridiculously overpaid profession. I had had fun with my sideline of inventions, I had made enough money, I knew an adequate number of people. That, I suppose, constitutes a sort of happiness. At any rate, I was willing to continue indefinitely along those lines.

But I wasn't fooling myself. I could get into serious

trouble this morning. It was not inconceivable that I could be charged with and convicted of the murder of Severance Flynne. The circumstantial evidence, once it became known, could be twisted all sorts of ways. The photographic proof of my innocence was missing.

The curse of an imagination is that you not only picture the worst results of a situation fraught with danger, you elaborate upon them. I saw myself in the courtroom, target for jeering eyes and bladed tongues. *Why did you kill a harmless man like Flynne? He never hurt anybody in his life. It was deliberate murder without provocation. You didn't shoot him? We shall prove, your honor, that the accused had the murder weapon in his possession. We shall show that he attempted to hide that fact. We shall produce witnesses who saw him go to the victim's room shortly after the death. We shall ask what happened to this so-called proof of his innocence. He had the film. We have no reason to assume that it was stolen from him. Why did he destroy it? Was it because it showed him killing that good and harmless man, Severance Flynne? Was it?*

Please omit flowers.

I saw myself in the death house, waiting for proof that never came. Waiting day after day, listening for that rush of footsteps, that jubilant voice announcing my innocence. Whose voice? My lawyer's, no doubt, for my friends would have deserted me.

I was not gay.

Nor was Riegleman, as he called the principals together like a referee before a fight. His dark eyes were sullen, and his long face was grim. But he had decided, apparently, to carry on in the best fashion. If the scene was to be retaken, it must be good.

"You may remember," he said, "my instructions of yesterday. These pioneers are threatened with death, and I want the audience to know that. The attack by Indians is not a dress rehearsal. Those Indians want scalps, and money, and guns, and horses. You will die if they succeed. You will die luckily if an arrow finds your heart; otherwise, you will die at their pleasure. This is not make-believe, and you must make the audience believe it."

He turned to me. "George, you feel certain that your band is strong enough to throw off the attackers, and the thought of defeat is secondary in your mind. Foremost in your thoughts is Carla. You mean to have her. She knows it and exults within herself, for you are Hilary Weston. As I told you yesterday, you will not let your inner fire die down, even in moments of extremity. You see your men fall, you see your wagons fired by blazing arrows, you are grazed across the cheek by an arrow, yet this fight is only a hindrance to the prosecution of your suit with Carla. You send her husband into danger with calculation. But here is an important point. You don't really care whether he is killed or not. If he is, that would be convenient. But you will have Carla, even if you have to kill him yourself. Is everything clear?"

We took our places, after stand-ins had done their bit, and the scene was ready to be shot. I put the events of yesterday and thoughts of my fate from my mind. They were of the past and of the future. I became Hilary Weston, and sight of Carla roused a flame in me. But I could not put Peggy Whittier from my mind.

Sammy was beside her, all right, putting questions to her. She checked her notebook now and then, and when her plain little face turned toward me, Sammy brought it back with a query. Sammy was doing his part.

Riegleman, Curtis, Paul, and a couple of electricians were a scattered group around that focal point. I noted them in passing, and fastened on Peggy. I could feel her eyes on my guns, even though I could see they were not.

"I'll give a rotten performance," I told my horse. "But maybe you'll be good."

Cameras began to turn, and I began to ride back and forth as the red horde poured over a sand dune toward us. I shouted my orders, I gave Carla a significant glance as I sent Frank out to die. When the raiders began their bouncing merry-go-round about our circle of wagons, I wrote *finis* to a life with each historic shot from my guns.

Any moment now, Peggy would stop the picture and point out that my guns were wrong.

The scene went on. Leather-fringed and feather-trimmed figures fell inside and out of the circle to lie uncomfortably in that blaze of sun until they could have lunch. The flat, staccato fire of the short rifles shattered the desert's ancient peace. I flung passion at Carla and lead at redskins.

Now the climax of the scene approached when the tide turned and carried away the ignoble redmen, while we pelted them with pellets of death. Cameras had turned for almost ten minutes now, and still they went on. No sign from Peggy. I began to play my part as if Hilary Weston were a man of blood and lust, not straw and brick.

Was it possible that Peggy had for once missed an important detail? I began to hope.

If she allowed the scene to run its course, the odds were in my favor that nobody would notice the discrepancy. Riegleman wouldn't. He didn't care for physical detail. His pictures were built around psychological detail. Sammy would notice, but that was all right. Curtis wouldn't notice; his attention would be on camera angles, photographic excellence, etc. The electricians would concentrate on light and shadow. The projector would probably read a book while the film ran.

Then, when the picture was released, an occasional amateur comedian would drift into the studio asking why I changed guns between shots. But by that time I hoped to have nailed the killer.

And so I began to hope, and consequently to play the part as if I meant it.

The moment arrived when I was to face the camera—represented by Carla on the screen—and express passion in the midst of danger. I was so caught up in the part that I didn't remember that this was the instant of Flynne's death on the day before. I faced the big black box, with my eyes on Peggy Whittier, and registered.

I saw her throw up a warning hand. She was about to stop the scene. Then she pulled her hand down, flattened its palm against her mouth. She stopped what she was about to do, and fear screamed from her eyes. Then she toppled forward, out of her chair, face down in the sand.

I spurred my horse and rode out of the scene.

This unexpected act sent him into a mild series of jumps which kept me busy staying on him. I sawed the reins, gripped with my knees, and forced him toward the camera. Finally, I half jumped and landed running.

Riegleman met me. "What the hell are you doing?" he shouted above the din.

I pointed behind him. He looked and fell in behind me. Between Peggy's shoulder blades was a circle of blood, slowly spreading on her organdy blouse. She was dead.

Chapter Fifteen

SOME SIX HOURS after Peggy's death, I was in jail.
It was not, the sheriff told me in my cell, really
an arrest. I wasn't to be charged with anything.

"Tell him what it is, Lamar," Callahan urged.

Lamar James allowed the corners of his thin mouth
to twitch. "No need to stand," he told me. "Relax.
Sit on your bunk." I did so, and he went on, "Look,
Mr. Sanders, we know a couple of things. We know
that Miss Whittier must have seen something yesterday. The way I put it together is this. She didn't at-
tach any importance to what it was she saw; she didn't
know that she had seen the murderer. But when that
point in the scene was reached today, she remembered.
You say she flung up a hand, and then put it to her
mouth like she was afraid. And the killer knew what
was going on in her head, so she got a slug in the
back."

"If I hadn't messed around with that film," I said
bitterly, "she'd still be alive."

"Not necessarily," James protested. "The killer
knew that she knew something. She'd have thought

of it sometime, and she'd have had to die just the same."

"It's my fault that she's dead," I insisted. "And I'll see that her killer dies for it if it's the last—"

"Now that's part of why you're in jail, Mr. Sanders."

"Call me George."

"Okay, George. Now, you were looking directly at her when she got it. The shot came from a point along your line of vision, extended beyond Miss Whittier. You can be certain that the killer saw that; he has an eye for detail. And it's no secret that you're messing around in this case. So all right, what happens? He may think that you saw something—like Miss Whittier—that would lead you to him. So you're next on his list. So this is a protective arrest."

"Your solicitude is a thing of tender beauty," I said. "I shall note it in my memory book."

"You can get sore if you like. But this is a legal move, and we can hold you."

I stood up. James's brown eyes didn't waver before mine. "There were a couple of hundred others out there, any one or all of whom could have seen what I did. Why single me out of the ruck?"

He gave me a sly smile. "I might as well put my cards on the table, George. I told you last night that I know you're hiding something. I don't like it. I almost arrested you then. But this is a better pretext than illegal parking, and it'll give us a chance to have a little talk."

"I told you I'd talk to you any time."

"Words," James said. "Just words. When I ask you

direct questions, you fluff me off. I'm going to get the truth from you even if I have to bring in a lie detector."

I looked at Sheriff Callahan. I felt again that the big man couldn't be depended upon to act rationally. He was in charge, but Heaven only knew what he might do under any given circumstances. I could talk to James; I could give him sincere evasions. He'd think them over before acting; he wouldn't get angry. But Callahan—

"Sheriff," I said, "I'd like you to be the first to benefit from an invention of mine. The lie detector brought it to mind. I'm working on a dingus that will make the lie detector seem like a kerosene lamp. The main problem of a peace officer is not to detect lies. Your own grandmother will lie herself blue in the face if she feels like it."

"My grandmother's dead," Callahan said seriously.

"A ouija board would prove me correct, then. But I didn't mean any specific person. My point is that everybody tells lies. You don't need a gadget to determine that. This person lies to her husband, this one to her lover, this one to his wife, this one to the whole country via radio or newspaper. A lie detector only indicates a condition which you knew existed all along. A criminal detector is different."

He frowned. "What do you mean?"

"That's what I'm working on. I'm using the old principle of the divining rod. Now we know, scientifically, that emotions cause an irradiation of detectable essences. Witness the dog. He senses that you're afraid, so he bites you. If you're not afraid, he goes back to his avocations, whose name, of course, is legion. A dog is busy, busy, busy."

"Sure is," Callahan agreed. "Had a dog when I was a kid, always into something. Hen houses, stables, living room, kitchen, drank soup off the table if you turned your head. My old man got drunk once and decided we didn't need a dog. So he lashed old Shep to a roasting pan, slathered him with bacon grease, and started to roast him in the oven. Would've, too, only Mom smacked him with a horseshoe the old man carried around in his pocket for luck. Shep spent the rest of the day licking off bacon grease, having a hell of a time. After that, every time he saw a rope, he'd try to find a pan to lay down in."

I veered him back to the subject, while Lamar James gave me a fishy stare.

"You're a keen observer, Sheriff, and have a remarkable memory. Just the type to use the criminal detector to the utmost. As I say, it works on the divining rod principle. We establish an electrical field around a pointer which is connected to a dial that fits in your lapel. Now you may walk along using this pointer as a swagger stick, keeping one eye on the dial, of course. If you don't get killed in traffic, you will see the variations on the dial. Here comes a girl in a red dress, say. As she passes, the needle just quivers, gently. She has criminal tendencies, but they are suppressed by her desires for attention—the red dress proves that. Now you approach a man in a derby hat; the needle doesn't move. He's probably a junk dealer. Ah, but now we see something! That little man scattering bread crumbs to the pigeons sends the needle zinging against the pin. Here is an arch criminal. So you don't ask him any questions; you toss him in the clink and beat hell out of him. Eventually he confesses to being head of a narcotics ring, and gives you the names of his confederates. You call in the FBI, give your information and prisoner to them, and receive a congressional medal. You'd look well in a congressional medal, Sheriff. You deserve one. It isn't every small town sheriff who breaks up a gang that has brought insomnia to G-men by the gross."

"I hate dope," Callahan said. "Ought to be stamped out, anybody handles it ought to be killed. Where is this here criminal detector? How much does it cost?"

"I'm going to make you a present of the first one," I said, "as a token of admiration and esteem. If you will go to my trailer, you'll see an ornamental knob on a panel to your right just as you enter. Turn that knob to the right, and the panel drops down to reveal a desk. In the upper right pigeonhole you'll find a set of drawings. If you'll bring them to me, I'll put in the finishing touches, and you can have a criminal detector in a few days. Think of it! Just by walking around, you can weed out the undesirables in your community. Ship them across the county line, and you'll have the cleanest little city in the world."

"Well, it sounds kind of screwy, but then you're an actor. I'll give it a whirl, though. What can I lose? See you later."

The sheriff went out, carefully locking the door behind him, and Lamar James frowned at me. "That's a hell of a way to treat poor old Jerry. He's really a good guy."

"I have no doubt of it," I said. "But if I talk, I want to talk to you alone. I know how you operate, but the sheriff baffles me."

"Okay, talk."

"I want to make you a proposition."

"Shoot."

"I want to give a party here tonight, and invite a select list of guests."

"What the hell are you talking about?" he demanded. "A party! What do you think this is, a dormitory?"

"I can't understand why you should object. You tell me I'm not actually under arrest. I'm more or less a guest. Why can't I ask my friends in to see me?"

"But in a jail!" he said.

"Home is where the heart is," I said. "What difference if it's jail or Chattanooga?"

"Who ever heard of a party in jail? What would people say?"

"If it turns out to be a good party, they'll probably say they wish they'd been there. Is there a law?"

He pondered. "No, not that I know of. But nobody ever gives parties in jails."

"Then we establish a precedent. Who knows, maybe it'll become a fad. 'Mr. Spike Donovan requests the pleasure of your presence on Thursday at 8 p.m. Black tie. Cell 26, Block B, Tier 4. R.S.V.P.' I like it. Jails need gaiety. Maybe we could work up a revue. The Ball & Chain Beauties. Or the Jailbird Jamboree. Music by the Arson Eight."

"What's the reason for this party?"

"On the surface," I said, "it's to wish Peggy Whittier hail and farewell. Best wishes for whatever, if any, the future may hold for her. She'd want it," I lied. "She was that kind of person. That's the on-the-surface reason. The real reason is to trap her murderer."

He slitted his eyes thoughtfully. "How do you expect to do that?"

"Psychology. Whoever killed her must have murder on his mind. We trap him into revealing it. Then we make the arrest."

"You make it sound good," Lamar James said bitterly. "How do you do it?"

"Wait until the party. I don't want you to know about the method. Then you'll be convinced when it happens."

"I haven't said there's going to be a party. Listen, why don't you mind your own business? Why don't you let me run this killer to earth?"

"I'd be glad to," I said. "Can you? What have you accomplished so far?"

"Damned little," he admitted ruefully. "We know all about Flynne now, and so far as I can see nobody had a motive for killing him. He was just a nobody. He didn't have dough, he had no prospects of getting any. He wasn't running around with any particular woman. His friends weren't intimate with him, and vice versa. He didn't bother anybody, he has no criminal record. He's worked at little jobs all his life. Nobody could have wanted him dead, as far as we can determine."

"Yet somebody did."

"Well, we know it was one of about three hundred people."

"You can narrow it to a dozen."

"The hell!" he exclaimed. "How?"

I explained my theory that if Flynne's killer had been an actor or an extra, he or she wouldn't have dared being caught by the camera. "Therefore," I said, "the only possible killers were those behind the camera. These include Paul, Sammy, Riegleman, Miss Nelson, Curtis, the nurse who bandaged my head, the boom crew, a couple of electricians, and a couple of people in the wardrobe department. You can eliminate some of those theoretically. The electricians and the boom crew were busy. Still, one of them could have stepped away for a few seconds and fired the shot, so we'd better include them as suspects." I paused and added, "I'd be willing to wager that if we could find and develop that stolen reel of film, it would prove I'm right."

"Now why didn't I think of that?" he asked in disgust. "Here I've been running over the whole personnel and going nuts. You can get your teeth into a few people, but a flock of 'em only get in your hair. That was nice work, George. I wish I could see that film."

I didn't wish he could see it. He'd see the guns. Which brought up a point. "By the way," I said casually, "how about prints on that gun we found in the wagon?"

"Clean," he said. "Somebody wiped it. Not a print. But you were right. The bullet didn't come from that gun. I want to know how you knew."

"If I trap the murderer," I said, "he'll tell you. Let me have a try, like a sport."

"It's okay with me, I guess," he said slowly. "You're

smarter'n I thought. Maybe you can get somewhere. I'll have to sell Jerry on the idea, though he's gonna be sore when he finds nothing in that desk."

"He'll find a set of drawings, just as I told him."

James's eyes widened. "You don't mean that was on the level, that criminal detector?"

"Why not? It's possible."

"We could use one now, all right," he said gloomily. "Nobody saw a thing. Everybody accounted for his movements at the time of the murder, and had at least one witness to back him up. Well, maybe this party will uncover something."

"Will you deliver the invitations?" I asked. "And there is one other thing I'd like before the party gets under way. I'd like to see Peggy's notebook. It had every detail of what was going on. Maybe we can find what caused her to remember."

He frowned. "Notebook?"

"Yes. You see, she recorded costume detail, location of this and that—anything and everything she saw. If a scene was interrupted, then, the director only needed to consult her to take up the scene again exactly as and where it was interrupted."

"Do you mean a copy of the script?" James asked.

"No, it was a notebook. Black leather, loose leaf."

"Then somebody took it," James said. "Because she didn't have any notebook when I got there."

This was a blow. A blow to my ego more than anything else. "I'm a half-wit," I said in disgust. "Of course there wouldn't be any notebook. Whoever killed her took it, because it had a clue at least to his identity. All we needed to do was search everybody immediately and arrest whoever had it. I suppose it's been burned by now."

James was suddenly flushed with anger. "I'm getting damned tired," he grated, "of learning important facts when it's too late. You didn't tell me about that film, and it was stolen. You didn't tell me about the notebook, and it's gone. There's something fishy here, and I want to know what!"

"You admitted the party was a good idea," I reminded him. "Let's get it started."

"All right!" he snapped. "But if anybody else goes haywire because you're holding out, God help you. I'm not kidding, George. You're not playing square. I think you're acting this way because you think it's best. Okay. I don't think you're a dope. But if this party don't get us anywhere, you're going to come clean, or I'll charge you with obstructing justice and you'll see what the state prison looks like from inside!"

Chapter Sixteen

I CLAIM NO FLAIR for philosophy that probes the hidden springs of human behavior. I am inclined to observe surface manifestations and deal with those. I have found this to be practical.

So, even now, when Peggy, who was something of a friend, had been shot in the back, I did not run down my list of suspects in search of basic motivations. The motive was there on the surface, clear as a signpost. The murderer knew that she had seen something—an act, a gesture, any abnormal characteristic—and made a note of it. He had to kill her to prevent her tagging him.

My plan to identify him was also a surface measure. The killer knew that he had committed murder. The very word *murder* must lie close to the surface of his consciousness. My purpose, then, was to jolt him into revealing that fact, and my plan to do so was simple.

I had "invented"—the term isn't strictly accurate, but suffices—a word game which had brought me many free drinks, and cost me a few, too. It began one day in the Derby bar where I ran into a highly literate lady who plays moronic roles on the screen and stage. I bet her a dollar I could give her three letters of a word, and she could not fit those letters into a word—mine or any other—within fifteen seconds.

"C-x-q," I said, and pushed the timer on my watch.

She turned on that mournful expression that has brought belly laughs to millions, and said "quincunx" in a voice that said I was pumping her heart's blood into the street.

"There isn't any such word," I said.

Heartbrokenly, she offered a wager of five dollars more that such a word existed, and the bartender offered to back her judgment with two dollars of his own. We adjourned to a near-by book shop, where she proved that "quincunx" concerned an arrangement of objects by fives, and I was eight dollars out of pocket.

I didn't play the game with her any more. I managed to recoup my losses from less erudite persons, and played the game occasionally off and on for two or three years.

Now, on the heels of Peggy's death, I wanted to get as many suspects as possible together and throw them letter combinations like d-m-u for *murder,* l-l-g for *killing,* m-h-c for *homicide,* and the like. It seemed to be a sound theory to me. Although it would prove nothing, it would concentrate my attention on the person who was self-conscious about coming up with any of those, or related, words, and we could investigate his alibi, motives, former associations with Severance Flynne, etc.

I hadn't speculated on Melva Lonigan's reaction to my being in jail.

She came rocketing in with Fred and a middle-aged stranger. She said, "They can't do this to me. Where's that half-witted sheriff?"

"Can't do what to you?" I asked.

"Put you in jail. What else?"

"I tried to tell her," Fred broke in, "that this is swell publicity for you. I think we ought to leave you here."

Melva's green eyes sparkled. "And does he make any money in jail? Not for me, he doesn't. I'm going to get him out."

"Go away," I said. "All of you."

Melva pushed a red lock off her forehead. "Now don't get hysterical, George," she said, as if to a three-year-old.

My voice went up in spite of myself. "Hysterical? You two ghouls have already done irremediable damage. You flocked in on the heels of a bullet and prevented me from finding who fired it last night. As a result, poor Peggy Whittier is dead. And now, when I make a simple request, I'm hysterical! Now go away! I mean it."

"You just don't know what's good for you," Melva said. "Your attorney will confirm that. Won't you, Mr. McCracken?"

The middle-aged man looked judicial. "The Constitution is being violated on three separate counts as long as you are incarcerated, Mr. Sanders. Surely, as good Americans, we cannot allow such sacrilege?"

He was tall, rather lean, very distinguished, with a touch of gray at his temples; the lower half of his face was a lighter shade than his tanned forehead, and he was a complete stranger to me.

"My attorney?" I said. "I didn't hire an attorney."

"Oh, yes," Melva corrected. "I did it for you. We can't let you rot in a louse-infested cell."

"Any lice in this cell," I said pointedly, "came from outside, since I've been here. I don't want an attorney. I have as much use for one as a second nose. I like it here."

"Atta boy, George," Fred said. "We can hit the front pages with this one."

"As for you," I said balefully, "you're my ex-press agent. I told you I didn't want any story about my working on this crime. I'm through with you."

"You can't fire him!" Melva said stoutly. "I've got a contract with you, and he's my fiancé. I'll admit he seems to have a head full of curdled milk at times, but what he did he did in your own interests."

"I can fire you, too!" I said. I'm afraid this approached a shout.

"Ah?" she said sweetly. "I'll sue you, my sweet, and wear a bathing suit in court. Do you think any jury would listen to you when I'm in a halter and shorts? And I'll tell 'em you stole the rest of my clothes, and you'd have taken my bathing suit too if you'd known where you could sell a used one." Her tone became soothing. "Let's don't fight, George. We like each other too well. This is for your own good, honestly."

"I refuse to argue," I said. "I want you to go, and stay away. You're unwelcome here tonight."

I turned my back on them, and looked stolidly at my bunk. Much to my surprise, Melva, Fred, and McCracken went silently away.

I sat on the stool, and heaved a small sigh of relief. The party would take place after all. I would conjure up a chief suspect by clever manipulation of word hints, and persuade Lamar James to let me go back to my trailer with its built-in inner spring mattress. I could turn the case over to him and get a good night's sleep.

Concentrating on this, I didn't hear Sheriff Callahan until he spoke with bovine heartiness in my ear.

"Well, sure was a short stay," he said, busily twisting a key in the lock. "Here's the plans you told me about. You can finish 'em anywhere you want to now."

He gave me the folder, and left the door open. He beamed down at me.

"Have you caught the killer, then?" I asked.

"Nope," he said cheerfully. "But we will. And there's no call to keep you any longer. Nobody thinks you done it."

"But I'm under protective arrest! My life is in danger."

"Shucks," he said. "Nobody's gonna bump you off. Even if they do, we'll catch 'em. Lamar's awful smart that way. So you got no call to worry."

"I'm not going out of here," I said. "I'm staying."

"Now look, Mr. Sanders," he cajoled. "You can't stay. I can't afford to get into no trouble with the federal men. They don't like the Constitution to be— uh, flouted, I think. Your lawyer was very nice about it, and I see where we was hasty."

"That nitwit isn't my lawyer, Sheriff. I tell you I have a plan to catch the murderer. All I want to do is have this party tonight, and I'll turn him over to you."

"Party?" Callahan echoed in astonishment. "What party?"

"Didn't James tell you?"

"Nope. He got a hot lead and went out on it."

I explained about the party. Sheriff Callahan was scandalized. "Not in this jail, you don't! What would the voters say if they heard about a Hollywood wild party in my jail? Sam Jenkins—he's the one who'll run against me next election—would make my jail sound like Sodom and Gomorrah before the fire. Never heard of such a thing. You get out of here or I'll run you in." He scratched his head. "Can't do that, though. You beat it now, Mr. Sanders. I don't want no trouble."

"If I don't go what'll you do? I'm as big as you are. I don't think you can put me out."

He laid a hand on his gun. "I reckon I can."

"You wouldn't dare shoot me. Think of what the voters would say about that. Sheriff Callahan makes an arrest, then drives the prisoner away at the point of his gun. Would you vote for a man who couldn't make up his mind? Would you?"

He was unhappily silent for a moment. Then, "Dang it," he said slowly. "All I know is you got to go." He was quiet for another long moment before his small eyes lighted happily. "You might as well go because, look, I won't let none of them people in to your party. Maybe I can't run you out, or throw you out, or drive you out, but I can sure as hell keep *them* out. So you'd just sit here by yourself."

I stood up. He had me there, all right. I walked out.

"So long," he called after me. "Maybe next time you can stay, huh?"

Melva, Fred, and McCracken awaited me on the sidewalk. Melva laid a slim hand on my arm and rolled beseeching eyes at me. "George, for your poor mother's sake at least, please go straight from now on."

I shook her hand away. "Perhaps somebody will explain this fourth-rate comic routine. Who is this oaf? I never heard of a lawyer named McCracken."

"He isn't a lawyer," Melva explained. "But he played one in *Jackleg*. Very good, too."

"I was only too glad," McCracken said in a deep voice, "to sacrifice my hirsute *decor* in the interests of justice, Mr. Sanders."

"Don't let him kid you," Melva said. "He was glad to scuttle his beard after he knew he'd still get his twelve-fifty per diem."

"All right," I sighed. "I give up. What are you talking about?"

"Mac was a beard," Melva said. "But I told him you'd pay his salary for the duration of the picture if he'd shave and get you out of jail."

I stared. I didn't trust myself to speak. She'd got me out of a jail where I wanted to stay, and saddled me with an ex-extra's salary.

"Of course," Melva added, "I get my ten per cent. Mac, you'll net only eleven twenty-five."

"I understand," he said.

"Let's go eat," Fred proposed. "You must be hungry, George, and anyway I want to talk over an idea. Look, say we give the papers the story that you'll produce this murderer next Sunday—"

"And invite everybody to tea?" I asked. "You people be off on your own affairs. I can't afford to be seen with you, and I mean that literally."

A car with a county license plate slid in to the curb. Lamar James shut off the ignition and lights, and joined us on the walk. "What are you doing out?" he asked me.

I told him, in short, smoking words. He grinned.

"It doesn't matter. I think I've got the killer. I'm going to pick her up in a few minutes."

"Her?" I said. "Who?"

"Wanda Waite. This Peggy Whittier had a room at Mrs. Holman's. This evening, right after dark, Mrs. Holman saw a female sneak into Whittier's room. I went out there and didn't find anybody, but I found Wanda Waite's prints all over the room. It's a little too coincidental to find 'em in Flynne's and Whittier's rooms both."

"Let me give you a friendly warning," I said. "Wanda didn't kill Flynne, and therefore had no reason to kill Peggy. Don't climb out on a limb."

"Don't worry," he said. "I'm picking her up for questioning. I've worked out a way to question effectively. As you may find out if I'm wrong on this."

He nodded pleasantly and went into the building.

Chapter Seventeen

"GEORGE, OLD BOY," I said to myself," the best thing you can possibly do is to stay out of this, beginning now. You have tried three ruses to trap this killer. You have rued each ruse. You have concealed evidence, you have allowed yourself to be placed in a position that is untenable and dangerous. You have directed suspicion at your friends. You have lied to constituted officials. If your snide part in this investigation becomes known, some judge will heave the book at you. But if you go back to the luxurious loneliness of your trailer and go to bed, your part need never to be known—if you stay in bed. You can plead leprosy, or that you were taken suddenly drunk, or that you are tired of being an actor and have taken up hypochondria. Come now, act as if that skull stuffing isn't frantic butterflies."

I waved vague dismissal at Melva, Fred, and Mc-Cracken, and followed Lamar James.

Sheriff Callahan bristled at me. "I thought I run you off, Mr. Sanders. Now, I don't want no—"

"I'm a visitor," I said. "This is unofficial. Where's James?"

Callahan waved at a corridor. "He went back to his lab. He's fussin' with microphones and stuff."

"Microphones? What does he do, record conversations?"

"Naw," Callahan said in disgust. "He's lookin' at bullets through 'em."

I went back to the laboratory, which was small, neat, and impressive. Lamar James had his eyes glued to a comparison microscope, eying two battered chunks of lead.

He looked up, frowning. "They didn't come from the same gun," he said, "but they came from the same make. Probably a pair of Smith and Wesson thirty-eight Specials. Now, why didn't he use the same gun?"

I decided, in a flash of idiocy, to tell him what I knew, to "come clean," as he had asked. This police laboratory, in a half-horse town, instilled amazement and respect. Among the apparatus I could identify were: a set of white arc lights, a large camera on a tripod, a Leica minicam, a single lens microscope, a binocular microscope, the comparison microscope he was using, a spotlight, a fingerprint outfit, Bunsen burners, crucibles, pipettes, graduated glasses, test tubes, a small electric motor with an emery wheel and buffer, two types of balance scales, a shelf of chemicals, and several micrometers. If Lamar James was capable of using all these materials, he was a good man, much better equipped than I for criminal detection. I didn't know how to use half the stuff I saw.

My native caution asserted itself almost immediately. There was no point in leading with my throat.

"How do you know?" I asked. "About the guns, I mean."

He turned toward me and lighted a cigarette with lean, brown hands. "By the weight of the bullets, the number of lands, and the leed. The leed on both these bullets, in inches, is eighteen and three-quarters. This is a characteristic of Smith & Wesson thirty-eight Specials. The rifling twist is clockwise. The groove diameter is point-three-five-seven inches, and this is another characteristic of the S & W gun. The leed on three types of thirty-eights manufactured by Colt is sixteen inches, and the rifling twist is counter-clockwise. The groove diameter on Colts varies in the thirty-eights. The Special measures point-three-five-four, the automatic point-three-five-six, and the revolver point-three-five-four inches. So, you see we can say almost definitely that these slugs came from Smith and Wessons, and from two separate guns, as you can see if you'll compare them under the microscope."

He showed me how to adjust the eyepiece, and to rotate the slugs separately or together. The infinitesimal markings, left by the barrels, differed on each slug. They were not from the same gun. I could have told him so, because the gun that killed Flynne was out on a sand dune.

"This came out of Flynne's head," he said, pointing to the bullet on the left. "It was traveling fast, and wasn't deformed very much, because it went through a thin part of his skull at the temple. This one, from Whittier, must have hit a rib. But the characteristics are measurable."

I looked up. "What do you mean, lands and leed?"

"The lands are the smooth surface between the rifling grooves, and the leed is an expression of how far a land must travel before completing a circle. It may also be expressed by the angle of leed, or the angle which the land forms with the longitudinal axis of the slug. But I don't have that special measurement microscope, so I figure it in inches."

"How do you know all this?" I asked.

He waved at a small shelf of books. "Tables. All that dope is in the *Atlas of Arms,* by Metzger, Heess, and Haslacher. Also *Modern Criminal Investigation,* by Söderman and O'Connell. I do a lot of studying."

"In anticipation of crime waves?"

"I'm not going to stay in this place all my life," he said quietly. "I've never had very much so far, but I intend to get what I want. I want to have a crime laboratory of my own, and I want to know as much about the subject as anybody in the business. I own a lot of this stuff, paid for by washing dishes and stuff."

"You amaze me. I came in here to tell you what I know, but decided I'd find out what kind of a guy you were first. You'll treat what I have to say confidentially?"

"If you haven't committed any crime, George, you got nothing to fear."

"My first suggestion, then, is that you leave Wanda Waite out of the picture. She isn't guilty. She didn't kill Flynne."

"What was she doing in his room, then?"

"I don't know. I watched her through the closet

door, and I thought she was wiping her fingerprints off things."

"*You* watched her?" he exclaimed. "What the hell were you doing there?"

"Looking for a motive, of course. My principal interest was in *why* Flynne was killed."

"Did you find anything?"

"A newspaper clipping. I doubt if it means anything."

I told him about the clipping, and gave a fair verbatim account of the story.

"All we needed in this," he said, "was the English nobility. Suppose Flynne is a relative?"

"That can be checked. But I thought you had gone into his life to some extent."

"Yeah. He was a bachelor of no importance. That's all I could find out. Where does Wanda fit into this?"

"She talked to him on the train coming up here. She *says* for the first time. He told her that he came from Nebraska. He was on this job under false pretenses."

"I know all about that," James said impatiently. "How come you want to know *why* he was killed? I want to know who."

"We know the means," I said. "He wasn't strangled or poisoned, he was shot. We know that something like a dozen persons had the opportunity. If we can find a motive, we can make an arrest in five minutes."

"How would you go about finding this motive?" He paused, added with a touch of embarrassment, "I haven't had much chance to go into the psychological angle of investigation, but you seem to know what you're talking about. I'm really asking for information."

"When a man is murdered," I said, trying not to sound too pedantic, "the reason exists in the record of his past. If you can produce a complete record, you can point to the reason why this and/or that person would want to kill him. It's dull work, and the only way you can get the information is to ask those who knew him."

"The trouble with that," he said shrewdly, "is that at least one guy is going to lie to you. The murderer. All the others may tell you the truth, but not him."

"Granted. But the way in which the killer evades questions and his whole manner during questioning gives you ideas which can be developed. I'll admit that it isn't a sure-fire method, but it's part of a general investigational pattern. And here we have two persons who knew him. Wanda, for one. And Herman Smith, whose place he took."

I almost added that Carla had known Flynne well, but a sudden idea struck me. If I could only get James out of town, I could go ahead on my present line of inquiry without revealing my complicity in this mess. Yes, my complicity had been inadvertent and accidental at first, but it had become something else again. And although I admired and respected Lamar James, I had seen him lose his temper a couple of times and didn't want to chance his reactions to the truth.

I was perfectly confident that my own actions in this matter would not harm the official investigation, and I knew that if James could get any more information than we already had, it would help. It seemed logical that he could get information from Herman Smith.

"Smith," I went on, "was apparently a friend of Flynne. We can assume that he knows something—habits, other friends, and what not. Why don't you run down to Hollywood and see?"

He smiled wryly. "I'd like to, but this office doesn't pay traveling expenses for its deputies. This office isn't very well financed. The population of the county is thin, and the tariff can't be too high per capita."

"If I paid your expenses?"

"Sure, I could go under those conditions, but why should you?"

"Suppose we say that I'm curious, and a trifle angry. I've tried three perfectly good gags for tagging our killer. They were messed up through no fault of my own. But my attempts were based on the science of deduction. Let's say that I'm tired of deduction, and would like to see a little honest work. Since I can't get away myself, I'm happy to foot the bill for you."

After more conversation, he went off to get Flynne's address from Paul, and I went back to my trailer to think.

I had three possible angles of attack. One, to find the gun that killed Flynne and try to trace its ownership; two, to find Peggy Whittier's notebook and identify the clue to the killer; and finally to see Wanda and Carla. I felt that the key was there somewhere, in the mind of one or the other.

As far as the notebook was concerned, I felt that I had no chance. It was dangerous to the killer; he had undoubtedly destroyed it by now. Finding the gun presented difficulties, too. I couldn't go out at night with a flashlight; the crew who lived on location might see me. The killer might see me, and wouldn't I make a good target!

I had to admit that so far I'd been conspicuously unsuccessful at learning anything from either Carla or Wanda. Of course, that didn't mean that another attempt might not succeed. *The Saint* and *The Falcon* had always done well at prying information from lovely ladies. The same tactics might work this time.

On the other hand, I reminded myself, tomorrow was going to be a busy day. We were going to have to shoot that scene over again. The girls would need to be at their best, and they should have a good night's sleep. This was not pure altruism on my part, there was the important fact that I didn't want a nervous and overtired actress to ruin a scene of the picture in which I was the star.

George Sanders, actor, had a brief argument with George Sanders, detective. The former won.

After all, I too was tired. I too had an important scene tomorrow.

The gun, then; let's concentrate on the gun. It's out there on the far side of the dune. It and the pearl-handled Colt which McGuire will begin to raise hell about soon. There is no brush there, no cover of any sort. A search by day is impossible; by night, dangerous. Cover. A sand storm would offer cover. Well, then, we should have a sand storm.

This idea pleased me. I could have a storm written into the picture and plod through it to where Listless had thrown the guns. The wind machines could be so placed, under my direction, that they would blow the sand away at that spot. I would time my pace and distance so that I should arrive at the time when metal showed through the sand. Then I should stumble and fall realistically, stick the guns under my coat, and stagger on. Not even the killer would notice anything phony, even if he were looking directly at me.

I could see the scene in my mind's eye. Hilary Weston, the hated, admired, loved, intrepid, brilliant leader of his little band, struggling through the storm when all else was lost save his steel determination to win through. He staggers! Is he done for? Then so are the others, for he is the heart of his people. See how he struggles there in the sand! Observe his heroic efforts to stand once more. He's up! He's down! He's up! Sing your song of triumph, you hidden violins that play on the desert by God knows what means! Scream defiance, wind! Blacken, sky! You shall not deflect Hilary Weston from his destined path, you shall not prevent Sanders from getting out of this mess! *whee!*

A good scene. One to wring murmurs of compassion from the audience, and cheers from Sammy if I found the guns. And if I didn't find the guns? Then the Sanders mind would have to conceive another scheme.

Knuckles fell on my door in brisk tattoo. I jerked out of dreams of Academy awards and continued freedom from jail to invite the knocker in. It was Paul.

He seemed nervous. "Uh, hullo, George," he muttered.

"Spread it on the mohair," I invited. "Have a cigarette and a drink?"

"Thanks."

I fixed drinks, sat opposite him, and looked at him. His black eyes avoided mine.

"I—uh," he floundered.

"Yes?" I said. "What's the matter? Are you afflicted with termites?"

He raised his eyes. They seemed to hold a combination of defiance, anxiety, and a debonair determination. A neat trick, that, but they looked that way to me.

"Well," he began again. "It's a nice night, isn't it?"

"H'm?"

"Yeah. The fog's lifted. Say, how you getting along on this investigation?"

"We expect an arrest any moment," I said flippantly.

"Yeah? Well, look, you don't need to look any further. You can put the arm on me. I did it."

Chapter Eighteen

M Y FIRST REACTION was not: "The crime is solved, now we can go on with our business." My first reaction was to see red.

I have read more news stories than I can remember in which the alibi of the accused was that he didn't remember stabbing, shooting, garroting, burning, or beating to death his victim. "I saw red." I have sneered at such alibis. No more.

When Paul was making his announcement, we were sitting opposite each other, drink in hand, cigarette in mouth, about five feet apart. I was probably in motion by the time he had finished his confession. The next thing I remember was that Paul was shrinking away from a blow aimed at his face. He looked as though he were going to faint. The next thing I realized was that I was aiming the blow. I caught myself just as I started to swing.

I backed away. A mental haze cleared before my eyes, and I had a coherent reaction. "This," I thought, "is the rat who shot Peggy Whittier in the back. In the back, the rat. I should have killed him."

The fear began to leave Paul's eyes. He fumbled for

the cigarette he'd dropped on the floor. It was a couple of minutes before he spoke.

"What were you trying to do?" he rasped. "Kill me?"

"If I'd had a witness to your admission, you'd be fish bait by now," I told him. "I didn't think I could feel this strongly about anybody. But Peggy Whittier was a sweet, helpless sort of person, and she didn't have a chance. She never knew what hit her."

His black eyes widened, reflecting the wall lamps in bright gold dots. "I didn't—" he began. He broke off to assume an air of bravado. "So?" he snarled.

I began to be able to look at him objectively. I wasn't afraid of him; he wasn't much more than half my size. I knew I could handle him. I sat down.

"All right, Paul," I said quietly, "let's have the story. Why did you kill Flynne?"

"He was a grade-A bastard, that's why."

"How?"

"How?" He eyed the rivulet of his spilled drink. "Look, could I have some more of that? My nerves—"

"The condemned man drank a hearty meal," I said. "Not my liquor. You can't have a drop of— Oh, what the hell," I said. "Of course you can have a drink." I fixed it. "Now," I repeated, "how?"

"How what?"

"You said Flynne was a grade-A bastard."

"Well, he was."

"How?"

"My God!" he flared. "Don't you know what a bastard is? You've been around Hollywood long enough to know."

"I've never made a classification. Grade-A is a meaningless term to me."

"He was a throat-cutter. He spread rumors. Turn your back on him, you'd get a knife in to the trademark."

"An extra?" I scoffed. "An unknown who couldn't keep his board bill up to date? You pass for a big shot. How could his sort harm you?"

"There's plenty of ways," he said darkly. "I'd have been a producer if it hadn't been for him. I'd have owned my own company maybe."

"So? Tell."

He paused for a moment, sipped at his drink, which shook in his hand. "I had an idea once," he began. "It had to do with photographic backgrounds for animated cartoons. I had an in, too, at a cartoon lot, and I was ready to shoot the backgrounds. It was a terrific idea. I might have got an Academy award, I might have got screen credit, hell, I might even have got paid. So I made an appointment with the producer, and this rat Flynne beat me to it and sold him the idea. That's when I first wanted to kill him."

"You knew him before, then?"

"Hell, yes. All my life."

"Oh, were you raised in Des Moines, too?"

"Right next door," Paul said. "He broke my new bicycle one Christmas."

"I see," I said. "Tell me. Where's the gun you shot them with?"

"I'll turn it in," he said, with a touch of uneasiness.

I stood up again. I was relaxed now. I took his

empty glass. "Have another drink, old boy," I said. "It'll help you to lie more convincingly. Flynne came from Nebraska. He and Peggy were not shot with the same gun. Who are you covering up for? I think you'd better tell me the truth now."

"You're trying to trap me," he said, angrily.

I set down the bottle of flat soda and looked at him. "Trap you? You walk in here and say you did it. Trap you? Trap you into what?"

"Well, you don't believe me. You don't believe I slipped out of my office, hid behind the first-aid trailer, drew a bead on the bastard and gave it to him."

"Did you do that to Peggy, too?"

He looked at me with misery in his eyes. It ran down the slump of his shoulders and dripped off his fingertips. It generated itself into a cloak; misery lay across his back like a wet shroud.

"Oh, damn it to hell!" he said, and he was close to tears. "Damn the lousy thing to hell and gone! I didn't kill her, George. Why didn't I think of that?" He straightened his shoulders, not quite throwing off his cloak of misery. "Give me that drink. Never mind the soda. My nerves are shot."

"Will you tell me the truth?"

"I've got to, I guess." I gave him the drink. He gulped it, shuddered. "Listen, George, you're not trying to pin it on her, are you? She didn't do it, honest to God, she didn't!"

Naturally, I hadn't the foggiest notion which she Paul was referring to. And I was caught between my ignorance and my desire to know. If I asked him directly, he might not tell me her name. On the other hand, if I egged him on, let him talk, he might tell me things that would help, and he might continue to think I knew.

"Didn't she?" I asked. "How do you know?"

"Because she didn't care! She didn't give a damn about him any more. It was all over between them. You've got to believe me, George! Maybe the evidence does point toward her, but it was a plant. Somebody wanted her to be stuck for it. But, so help me, it was over more than two years ago. She hasn't even seen him until he showed up here to get murdered."

"How do you know she hasn't seen him?" I asked.

"Because she told me. I believe her. She wouldn't lie to me. We're going to be married."

"Congratulations," I said. "And so, to insure your happy marriage, you flip in here to confess to murder. Where were you intending to spend your honeymoon, in the gas chamber? A little stuffy, I should think."

"Hell, I don't know what I was trying to do. All I know is that I wasn't going to see her get stuck with it."

"What makes you think she was?"

He was beginning to relax now. The drinks were taking hold. "Well, I knew you were working on it, and I knew you could solve it. Listen, I've seen your pictures, and I've read all *The Saint* stories. Well, I didn't think much of you as an actor, but you were a hell of a detective. You couldn't make it so convincing if you weren't pretty good. So here comes this situation. I knew you'd nose around in the past, and uncover this thing. From there it was an easy jump. And the hell of it is, the evidence points to her. So, I guess I went off my nut. I thought if I confessed, I'd be tried but they couldn't prove it. Then they'd throw the case out of court, and by that time it'd be forgotten. So she could go on. She's got a great future, you know."

"Has she?" I prodded. "Personally, I think she's terrible."

He was on his feet instantly. "You can't say that about Carla. I don't give a damn if you are bigger than me."

I waved him back into his seat. "Carla, eh?"

His eyes widened. "Why, you dirty rat!" he cried. "You didn't even know who I was talking about!"

"Whom," I corrected. "Let's don't be sloppy."

"Ah, shuddup!" he growled. "Of all the stinking tricks." He tossed off the fresh drink I put in his hand. "The great detective! Was I ever a sap! You don't know from nothin', any more than I do."

"Not as much," I agreed. "You may as well tell me what you know."

"I'll tell you nothing!"

"I'll find it out, anyway."

"Go ahead. The hell with you."

"Carla was here," I told him. "She told me a fanciful yarn. Coupled with what you said tonight, it looks serious. Do you want me to go to the sheriff with it?"

"What'd she tell you?"

"Uh-uh. You talk."

He leaned forward earnestly. His eyes were beginning to take on a slight glaze. "What did she tell you, George? She don't know whass good f'r. Gimme—give —me anurr—drink."

I poured him a double shot. He stared into it for a long time, tossed it off. "Zhorge," he said, after a while. "Ole Zhorge." He put his head gently between his knees and passed out.

Chapter Nineteen

UNLESS YOU WEIGH 63 pounds in divers' shoes, you don't pass out on four drinks. Five, counting the double shot. Of course, liquor hits different persons different ways. It hits the same person different ways on different occasions. But you don't pass out.

So, he had primed himself before coming. The potions of liquid courage had formed an anesthetic foundation for the good scotch I had given him. I should imagine, too, that his subconscious had something to do with it. I was larger, heavier than he. I could have forced admissions from him. So he passed out.

I went through routine conventional moves to bring him to consciousness. I slapped his face, I pulled his black hair. I wiped Sticko off my hands and tickled him. It was like trying to revive a sack full of sand.

I remembered a story I had heard. Three campers had finished their evening meal of game that had seemed slightly high. One was stricken with ptomaine. He writhed on the ground, groaning like an attic ghost. The chef, wounded to the depths of his culinary sensibilities, took a boiling pot from the bed of coals and emptied it on the sufferer's stomach. The victim screamed to his feet and beat hell out of the chef, but the ptomaine was cured. Would this cure drunkenness?

I put a teakettle on my electric grill. When it was hot, I laid Paul on his back and opened his shirt. I poured a dollop of steaming water on the tender skin of his stomach.

No frightened gazelle ever moved faster from an ambushing lion. If the door of my trailer had opened inward, he'd have left a jagged outline of himself as he plunged through it into the night. His feet sped him instinctively away; in a few seconds, his yells were only a remembered earache.

A round face, with great dark eyes poked itself around the trembling door. Wallingford eyed me and the kettle, smoking in my hand.

"George!" Wallingford cried. "What you doing to that poor fellow?"

"I just poured a little boiling water on his stomach, Wally. Come on in."

"Thanking you just the same, George, I'm liking it here. I can duck."

I poured out the water, turned off the grill. "Come on. I was just trying to get some information from him."

He edged into the trailer. "I don't know from nothing. Don't even think question marks. I'll dream about his screams."

"He passed out," I said. "I was just bringing him to." I grinned at the fat little man. "Have a drink?"

"Not so long as I can fight you off. You will get

yourself in a cell with soft walls, George, doing things like that. Maybe you better take a few days off, huh? Maybe the strain is breaking you?"

"Let's just forget it," I said. "It wasn't very important. What's on your mind?"

He cast another apprehensive glance at the kettle, seemed to relax, and smiled shyly at me. "It's John," he said.

I blinked. I was a little dazed. "I'd never have thought it, Wally. Fancy! John."

"Nor lots of others, even," he said smugly. "I telephoned New York, and Al Williams, who should be knowing, guessed James and Jedediah. You should have heard me hang up in his ear. Guessing! I got no time for games. Even Sol Spatz in Hollywood said he thought it might be Jeffrey. So I called New York again."

"So far, that's about eighteen dollars worth of phone calls."

"But it's worth it, George. Now I know. I called the secretary of the Stock Exchange, and he said it was John. A good solid name, no?"

"*What* is John?" I demanded. "And don't give me an Oley Speaks' parody."

"The *J* in my name, what else? For J. P. Morgan. It was John Pierpont."

"You could have found out by calling the public library," I pointed out.

"But it wasn't open in New York."

"You could have wired one of the lions, then. Let's get off this vaudeville routine, Wally. I have an idea. We need a sandstorm."

"Not me, George. I got as much use for a sandstorm as a fish for a manger."

"I mean in the picture. Here we are on a desert. If we have to fight our way through a sandstorm, we'll be exhausted. Then if the redskins attack, our triumph will be all the more impressive. There's something mystical in it, Wally. The early pioneers were determined to win through and build up this country. Neither storm nor ambush, man nor nature, deters them. They fight to the last man, but that last man wins through."

"If we kill 'em all off," he reflected, "it saves money. All them extras cost as much as a couple good actors."

"I was speaking metaphorically," I said. "Or is it hyperbolically? I don't mean that only one man shall come through. I mean that the scene shall show the *intent* that at least one man shall come through. We have the evidence of that intent all about us in these latter days—buildings, roads, orchards, farms."

"And Hollywood," he added. "It's a good idea, George. It would show what people went through so we could have pictures and telephones. But we can't do it."

"Why not?"

He rose and seemed to tower in his rage. "Because we can't find the author! He leaves his agent's office for the studio, and nobody ever hears from him again! We got a scene to rewrite, and now this! I'm losing my mind. Murders, bad newspaper publicity, and no author yet!"

"He can't have just vanished."

"Claude Rains did, George. Right before your eyes on the screen in *The Invisible Man*."

"That was a trick."

"Maybe," he said moodily. "I wonder. Sometimes I think we really do these things, and are just kidding ourselves with trick talk. Now we got an author up in smoke. Better I should have stayed in pants and suits."

"He'll turn up," I soothed. "Who is this author?"

"Name's Arthur Connaught. A thousand a week we're paying him to be lost. It ain't practical."

"Maybe I can do something about finding him."

He scowled at me. "You don't find nobody. You try to find who killed that poor guy and we lose the master film. Then we lose a script girl, poor girl. Don't you try to find no author, George. We might even lose me."

Presently, he went off morosely and I went to bed.

Not to sleep, oh, no. I had yearned for this inner-spring mattress with every aching bone. I had thought to lose my worries in a cloud of unconsciousness. And the moment I hit the bed I was wide awake.

There was nothing I could do about ascribing a motive for Flynne's murder until James came back with biographical data, but I could think about it. I couldn't keep my mind off it. Where did Carla fit in?

So she and Paul were going to be married, eh? A slight wrench of disappointment twisted my insides. Carla wasn't important in my life, but I didn't like the comparison between me and Paul. From my own viewpoint, I was a more desirable character. So was he from his, I suppose.

Then a really terrific idea hit me. Paul *had* done it. He had killed Flynne, planted the gun on me, tossed my gun into Carla's wagon. He had played odds on that. If the murder weapon were found on me, I would be accused. If not, suspicion would fall on Carla when the prop gun was found. Then, knowing that she couldn't be convicted, he came and made a confession which could easily be proved false. This would take suspicion off him. He would be regarded as a dope, to be sure, but that was better than having a front page picture captioned "Convicted."

The hows and whys escaped me, but the psychological pattern was intact. Some time, somewhere, Flynne had incurred his enmity. Coincidentally, Paul had become attracted to Carla. He learned of their past relationship, which added fuel to his burning desire to rid the world of Flynne. And so he had waited. The opportunity came, and he seized it.

How cunning he was! He had worked out each step, and he had almost gotten away with it. Had it not been for my insomnia, he might have.

I smiled to myself in the darkness. It was all over now, all over but using facts which James would bring back. Then accusations, arrest, trial, conviction, death. I hoped it would be a painful one, for having shot Peggy in the back.

With this problem wrapped up in logic, I dismissed it and turned to the problem of my telephone. There must be a way to make it hang up. When the caller replaced his telephone, he broke the circuit. Now, suppose that the initial call should activate an electromagnet which caused my telephone to answer. The slight current flowing through the line while a conversation was in progress would hold my phone open. But when the call was terminated, the circuit broken, the field around the electromagnet would collapse. This would—

That was as far as I got. I began to dream of a waterspout at sea, full of authors named Connaught.

Sammy met me as I arrived on the set the next morning. "Did you die?" he asked. "You're ten minutes late."

"I woke up in the middle of a dream. I had to go back to sleep to finish it."

"Hurry and get made up," he urged. "Riegleman is in a foul mood. Everybody's waiting on you."

I dashed to my dressing room and sort of hurled myself into my togs. I buckled on my guns and went out to face the camera.

We had a new script girl, with a brand-new notebook. Still, the chair seemed empty. I saw Peggy there, how she had flung up her hand, jerked, fallen.

We took our places at the point where I had broken the scene yesterday. Riegleman started to give the signal to begin, but halted to glower at me.

"Where did you get that bloody cravat?" he yelled.

I dismounted and walked over to him. The new script girl smiled at me. She was pretty, small, and dark. I winked at her. "In my dressing room," I said to Riegleman. "What's the matter with it?"

"Nothing, George," he said gently. "It's excellent. Only it happens not to belong in the picture. Yesterday, you wore a black string tie. We ran through most of the scene. Now we resume the scene, to find you in an Ascot. Surely somebody would ask how you changed ties while dodging bullets?"

"You're right," I said. "I hadn't noticed."

I changed ties, thinking how unlike Riegleman this was. He did not customarily say anything about detail. He left that to others. Nor was he usually so sharp and sarcastic. Still, he'd been set back hard these last two days. Two murders couldn't add to his serenity. They had apparently sharpened his powers of observation, though.

The Beard was waiting outside my dressing room. Not for me. Not for anything. He simply leaned against the side of the trailer and stared fixedly at nothing. He seemed tall and stooped even in that position.

"Hello," I said. "Sulking?"

He raised his flashing black eyes. "I cannot stand it," he said, gloomily. "I have never ridden a horse before. I never will again."

I looked at him in surprise. "You must have a poor excuse for an agent. Didn't he tell you you'd have to ride?"

"Never mentioned it," the Beard said. "If I'd known that was required, I'd never have taken the job. Mr. Sanders, I'm going back to Hollywood on the first train."

"Oh, come now," I said as cheeringly as I could.

"Don't give up so easily. Stick it out. Stout fella, and all that sort of thing."

He groaned, and shook his head. "At my age, I cannot get used to sleeping on my stomach. I didn't close an eye all night. I can't sit down, and I'm so tired from standing I can hardly see."

"I'm sorry," I said. I added, vaguely, "Cheer up," and went away.

I mounted my horse, and we took up the scene at a point shortly before the break of yesterday. I galloped back and forth, and when I turned to record passion for Carla on celluloid, I thought of Paul. I don't know what my expression was, but it certainly couldn't have been a burning one.

Riegleman blew his whistle. Action stopped. He walked over to me. "One does not ordinarily slit his eyes at his beloved," he chided me. "Love comes from eyes wide and clear. I'm sorry, George, old boy, but you looked as if you were ordering a bank cashier to hand over the loot. Shall we try it again? You are in love with this woman, George. Please remember."

I wondered if he came near the actual truth. When I looked at Carla, a little flame of triumph flickered in me. I was going to rid her of a louse.

We tried the scene again. Riegleman broke it off.

"George," he said. "You seemed frightened. Fear also shows in eyes wide open. Get some lust into your expression, man! This girl is worth fighting for, worth killing for!"

We tried the scene again. Same result.

"That's all today," Riegleman said in disgust. "Will you drop in on me later, George?"

Chapter Twenty

SAMMY AND MCGUIRE were a mildly arguing duo when I went into Sammy's office trailer. The property chief was frowning.

"Try to remember to bring 'em in tomorrow," he said. "Or here's a better idea. I'll stop in your room and pick 'em up this evening."

I broke in, to Sammy's evident relief. "Pick what up? I doubt if you'll be in your room today, Sammy. We've got to have a sandstorm, and I want to work out the scene with you. We'll have to do it ourselves, since we lost the author."

"Oh, yes," Sammy answered, as if he knew what he was talking about. "The sandstorm. Look, Mac, I'll try to remember to get those guns to you tomorrow, sure. Okay, George, let's get at it."

McGuire went away. Sammy asked, "What sandstorm?"

I explained my idea. He was enthusiastic, and went me one better. "That gives us a legitimate excuse to look the ground over. Maybe we can find the guns, and we won't need the storm."

We went to the stakes I had driven, and followed their direction to the big dune. Sammy sank to his ankles on each step and was soon shuffling like a locomotive. Neither of us commented on this. We were in no mood for wisecracks.

When we were out of sight of camp, that lonely immensity brought on a great depression. Here was the earth primeval. These dun wastes had lost their place in time. In arable land, time exists in the cycle of growth. Seeds take hold, sprout, mature, and die. Little streams grow wide in spring, dry in summer. Fledglings lose their down for more practical plumage, molt, mate, eat, fly, and die. The rhythm of caterpillar, cocoon, butterfly, marks the footstep of time.

Here was no life, no death, only an eternity of shifting, formless patterns. The wind came willynilly to shift one grain of sand from heedless relatives to heedless strangers. And along comes another wind to shift another grain of sand, and along comes another wind—and so on. Movement, yes, but not a time of life or death, of reaping or sowing, of weeping or laughter.

There was a time of weeping for us, all right. It arrived after we had sifted several truckloads of sand through our fingers. That wind which had moved the unknowing grains had also covered the guns beyond our poor power to detect or deduct their location.

"I give up," Sammy punch-lined. "Where are they?"

"Only the wind can tell," I said.

We stood there, burning under the sun, and flung lyrics at each other.

"Then speak with the tongues of winds," Sammy declaimed, "for this wind—this here wind—is dumb as hell."

"I shall speak with the tongues of wind machines," I answered. "Progress, machine age, and stuff. Sammy, we're insane. We've a touch of sun, I think. Let's go back to the jute chutes."

We trudged away. "Now what?" Sammy asked.

"I'll sell Riegleman on the idea. I'm to see him this afternoon. I think he's going to dutch-uncle me for bitching that scene. But I couldn't help it. I couldn't get my mind on the role."

Sammy grunted sympathetically. "You were looking at her when she keeled over."

We went on in silence.

The beards had all trooped off to dodge razors for another day, the principals and executives to whatever they do when nobody is looking, and only a scattering of technicians puttered about the wagons and trailers. A horse whinnied in his synthetic paddock, which had been placed down wind. I got off my make-up and went into town.

I stopped at the hotel to see Riegleman, and had Wallingford in my hair before I got out of the car.

"George, you got to do something again!" he babbled. "Better I was dead. One more is all I ask. Just one more. I will give Vesuvius cards and spades and make history. Well, *do* something!"

I took away his hand, which was wrinkling my coat.

"Please, Wally. Don't clutch. Who's been eating your porridge now?"

"You're right," he snapped. "Little Goldilocks yet. Somebody told the L.A. papers she was questioned *in jail!* Call that friend you call an editor and tell him for me—"

"Why didn't you tell him? She's your property, not mine."

"I told him. But he hung up."

"You've got to be gentle with editors."

"I'll be gentle!" he raged. "I'll buy him a new suit. A double-breasted libel, and that's my final word."

"One of these days, Wally, your vocal cords are going to leap out and flagellate you. I'll call him, so relax."

"Smith" gave me a mental hot-foot. "I killed the story the first time," he said, "because Wanda isn't very good copy. Mother Hubbards don't give any pulse a dirty beat, but boyohboy! We got a picture of the lady this morning in little more than a grin and gams. What gams!"

"Sucker," I said, rallying as best I could.

"Oh, yeah? Take a look at 'em sometime. Even if they were artificial I could get a glandular upset."

"Oh, she has legs," I admitted. "But are you falling for that old gag?"

"Somehow," he lyricized, "legs are ageless for me. They never grow old. Always there's freshness in the curve of a calf, the knife-edge of an ankle, the cornucopian flare of a thigh. I love 'em!"

"But as a newspaper man, you don't give columns

of space to publicity hounds. This is just a gag to get her in the public eye. You'll be a laughing stock—to Wanda."

"If she'll laugh at me in person— How do you know?"

"I helped her work it out," I improvised. "We were talking one night, and I advanced the theory that any actor could get publicity by departing from the role usually associated with him. If I should dress in missionary robes, God forbid, the fact in itself would get me in the rotogravure as long as I had some kind of a story to go with it. I didn't think she'd try to get mixed up in a murder just to test my theory. But I tell you this, chum. She had nothing to do with these murders. I give you my word of honor on that."

"Can I quote you?"

"Certainly. Will you call the other papers, like a pal?"

"If you'll give me the break on the solution. Hell, it isn't customary for one editor to call his competitor and warn the oaf against sticking his neck out."

"I'll give you the break," I promised. "When and if."

The explanation I had given sounded pretty good to me. I hung up and thought about it. Then I called "Smith" back.

"Where'd you get these stories?"

"We have a correspondent up there," he said. "He telephoned them in."

"Who is he? How can I find him?"

"I don't know much about him. He's sent in a few local items before. His name's Lazarus Fortescue."

"You're kidding. There isn't any such name."

"That's the way his checks go out, when we print anything of his."

"What does he sound like on the phone?"

"Like a cow-county correspondent. What else?"

"Thanks." I hung up and went to the desk, with Wallingford padding along spewing "Well?'s" at me. I brushed him off. The old desk clerk was plugged in on the switchboard. "Where will I find Lazarus Fortescue?" I asked.

He put down his headset. "Yup? What can I do for ya now?"

"Didn't you hear my question?"

"Heard my name. Answered, didn't I?"

"You're Lazarus Fortescue?"

"Ain't no *im*postor."

I dammed the tide of Wallingford's interrogation. "It's all right," I said. "It's fixed."

"George," he said, "you can be a son to me any day. I want to buy you a present for the end of the picture. Name it. Even if it costs a lot."

I paused and grinned at him. I knew Wally. If I asked for a private yacht, or a pet alligator, or a souvenir from Buckingham Palace, he'd see that I got it, now that he'd committed himself. It was a temptation I couldn't resist.

"Name it, George," he said again.

"All right," I said very casually. "I want a transit. A twenty-two inch achromatic."

He took out a notebook and started to scribble. "A *which?*"

I repeated it. Wally blinked, but he wrote it down.

"I'll see that you get it, George. Anything to make you happy."

"Now," I said, "will you go up to Riegleman's room and tell him I'm on my way? I want to get some information first."

He padded away. "Let's have it," I said to Lazarus Fortescue. "What about these stories on Wanda Waite?"

"Ain't stories," he said. "They're true."

"All right. Where did you get 'em?"

"Got 'em from her. She wouldn't lie about that. Might lie about other things. Most women do. Had a redhead once—Lies, you never heard nothin' like—"

"Did she ask you to telephone the papers?"

"Yup. 'N she got me to take her pitcher." He gave a low whistle. "I'm ready to go any time now, whenever the Boss upstairs calls me. Now I seen everything."

"Is she in her room now?"

He glanced at the key rack. "Yup. Goin' to see her?"

"That is my intention." I walked toward the stairs.

" 'F I could lose twenty years," he said, "I'd fight ya for her."

Wanda was not seductive now, except in the way that a lovely woman is normally seductive. She was in her quilted robe again, with her hair down. Her eyes narrowed a trifle at my expression as she invited me in. She waved me to a chair, curled up on the bed, and waited for me to speak.

I began slowly. "I've always had the greatest admiration," I said, "for detectives, amateur or otherwise, who could hide behind a closet door and see everything that was going on in a room. Aside from the danger that someone may open the door at any moment, it's incredibly difficult to see much through a half-inch crack. Try it yourself sometime, and find out. Therefore, I must ask you—"

Deliberately I paused, lighted a cigarette, and stared at her with the expression *The Falcon* invariably assumed while questioning a lovely woman.

"Just what," I demanded, "did you take from Severance Flynne's room?"

She looked at me coldly. "Nothing."

"You didn't take anything from Peggy Whittier's room, either."

She shook her head.

"But you left something there," I said. "On purpose, too. Fingerprints. All over the place. You did everything but write your name on the wall. And a very clumsy job of planting clues, if you ask me."

That brought her bolt upright. Her eyes widened. She said *"George—!"*

"I advanced an evasion this morning," I said, "to an editor. I gave him a fanciful tale. After I had finished, I had a hunch it might be true. I have discovered that it was. Tell me the truth, Wanda. You're messing around in a dangerous situation. I want to know why. Then I won't waste time wondering. Why did you send out those phony stories?"

"They were true," she said quietly.

"The implications were false. Why? And why this siren act, each time observers were present?"

She was quiet for a long time, her wide blue eyes

full of thought and—bitterness? Baffling expressions. Then she got to her feet, and took off her robe. She had on a white halter and shorts. She stood and looked at me.

I looked at her clinically, for that was the atmosphere. She was as casual as if she were showing me a ring. Appraisal was what she wanted, and I gave it. We said nothing.

She was stacked, as the boys say. She was assembled with an eye to lush detail. Her shoulders were firm, tanned, and straight. She was tanned all over, even, I suspected, under the wisps she wore. Her arms were long and tapered, her breasts full and joyous, her waist small, her stomach flat and hard, and her legs seemed never to come to an end. "Smith" was right. And Lazarus Fortescue had every right to dream his way into the grave after seeing this.

"Very pretty," I said.

She donned her robe. "Nothing wrong with it," she said. It wasn't a question. "I can stack this pile of bones up against any. And so what happens? The geniuses of Hollywood drape me in Mother Hubbards. I'm a missionary. I'm a minister's wife. When I'm supposed to turn on the heat, it's a charcoal stove. I'm sick and tired of being a good woman. I want to be bad!"

I waited. No sense in interrupting yet.

"You'll admit I can make blood bubble," she went on. "But I made the mistake once of trying out for a woman of good works, and they gave me the works. So I thought I'd change. If I could get into a jam, and not far enough to blackball me, maybe those limp-brained producers would consider me in another light. I'm a good actress. I can even do high comedy, and that's what I want to do. But you can't do drawing room dalliance in a shroud."

"You remind me of me, baby," I said. "It got so that every time I'd hear a car backfire, I'd automatically reach for a magnifying glass. I was typed, too. I broke away, but not by my own efforts." I paused. "You took that reel of film out of my trailer. Why?"

"It had proof of my innocence. It was my hole card. You see, George, I'm an amateur at being bad. So I thought that if I went too far, and was arrested in earnest, I could produce proof that it was just a gag."

"How did you know it was proof?" I asked.

She shrugged her shoulders. "I know where I was when Flynne was shot, and what I was doing. The same film that showed him falling dead would show that I didn't have a gun in my hands at that moment." She smiled wryly. "It sounds a little ghoulish, using the death of somebody as a springboard to top billing. But he was dead. I couldn't harm him."

"No, but you obscured the over-all picture. Well, I'll see what I can do for you after this picture is in the can. I sympathize with your feelings, and I think you're a fine actress. You deserve a break. Meanwhile, will you drop this nonsense and give me the film?"

"Sure," she said. "I'll be a good girl until the show is over. But then, by golly, I'm going to be horrid! It pays more, too!"

"It always has."

She went to the wastebasket, and rummaged. She rummaged and rummaged. She turned, white-faced.

"Somebody," she said quietly, "is trying to get me into *real* trouble. It's gone."

Chapter Twenty-One

O N THE NIGHT of Wanda's arrest, I had searched
this room. I had looked into and under everything but the ceiling flyspecks.

I looked at her speculatively. I told her about my
search. My eyebrows probably implied that she was
lying.

"I put it in the wastebasket that night," she said.
"It just fit in the bottom. It looked like a false bottom. I shoved it down good and firm so it wouldn't
fall out if the basket was emptied. Then I put back
what had been in the basket. Used Kleenex, empty
cigarette packages, old newspapers, just stuff."

I couldn't remember whether or not I had looked
in the wastebasket. I was under the impression that
I had not.

Super-sleuth Sanders!

"I'm a dope at times," I said. "All right, it's gone.
It behooves us, I think, to walk softly. Be careful,
and stop messing in this. Our killer is a dangerous
person. Lock your door when I go, and keep it locked
at night."

"That's no good," she said reasonably. "Whoever

it is knows me. We're probably friends. I cannot keep friends out."

She was correct. Either all persons were suspect, or none. She could hardly close her door against everybody.

I sighed. "I'm sorry that you got into this," I said. "But, since you did, it gains little to moan. Be careful, anyway."

I went to Riegleman's room, prepared to be lectured. When I was seated, and we had cigarettes going, he creased his high forehead with a frown and filled his blue eyes with unhappiness.

"I find myself in an unhappy position," he began. "An important reel of film has disappeared. Ordinarily that would not present such serious difficulties save that the retake is a body blow to the budget."

He paused. I felt slightly uncomfortable. That reel of film had been lost while I was responsible for it.

"However," he went on, "the notebook of my script girl has disappeared. As you know, George, it contains every important detail of action, costume, movement. We cannot risk the discrepancies. I see nothing for it except to retake everything. We had a three-day shooting schedule here. We have used it, and we have nothing except a long shot of the caravan filing across the desert at sunrise. Perhaps we can use that. I want to apologize for being finicky this morning, George. Ordinarily I remember nothing about the scenes except the psychological verities. I happened, just happened, to remember your tie. I am afraid I lost my temper."

"You had reason," I said. "I stank."

"Yes," he agreed, "you did. Also with reason. Both murders occurred while you were facing the camera. You couldn't help but remember Peggy stiffening with discovery, then going limp in death. Poor child. Which brings up another reason for retaking our scenes from scratch."

He paused, drilled me with eyes which lost their gloom. "Do you realize," he asked, "that the murderer must have been behind the first camera? His presence must have registered on someone besides Peggy. Unconsciously, perhaps. Nonetheless, somebody knows who he was, and a recreation of the scene as near to the original as we can manage might recall it to the mind of the person who knows."

"So now you're going to play detective?"

"As far as the death of that extra is concerned," he said grimly, "I am unaffected. I didn't know him. But I knew Peggy. That brings me into this as a person. I want to see her avenged. From the murderer's point of view, her death was necessary, and possibly he killed her with reluctance. But it was murder." He paused. "Somehow it only seems like *murder* when one knows the victim. That's why I have an idea that it might be pleasant to see that the murderer gets what he deserves."

"I like your idea," I said. "I have a few others of my own to supplement it. I agreed with you to stay out of this, but I gather that you won't hold me to that agreement, now that you are in it, too?"

His long face became stern for a moment, relaxed. "I can hardly ask you not to help find the murderer of Peggy. I want you to help me do something, George.

Before we retake that scene, we must speak to everyone we feel can be safely eliminated. We will ask them to try and remember, as the scene is being retaken, every minute detail they observed the first time. We can confer with each, privately, after the scene is finished. In that way, we may get a lead on the truth."

"Have you considered the cost on this?" I asked.

"Cost!" he snorted. "Would all the money in the world bring Peggy back? If a few dollars can lead us to her killer, they will have done more work than money usually does."

"Riegleman," I said. "I have misjudged you. I apologize."

He gripped my hand. "Thank you, George." He gave me one of his rare smiles as I went away.

I adjourned to a near-by bar to consider his proposition over a beer. Those whom I could surely eliminate were myself, Wanda, and—. And? Not Sammy. I was morally certain of his innocence, but I had no proof. Well, I could gamble on Sammy.

I shook my head in sudden disgust. Paul had done the killing. It remained only to trap him, and when Lamar James returned we would do that little thing.

Still, Riegleman's idea had merit. Surely somebody had seen the murderer. Perhaps he could be made to remember. Then who should be asked? Curtis? He was a nice little guy. Yes, Curtis. McGuire? He wasn't even near the scene. The electricians and boom crew, yes, and the sound men.

I was lost in the amber depths of my beer, oblivious to the three or four customers at the bar, and didn't notice Fred and Melva until I heard an unctuous admonition.

"But please don't call me Reverend, bartender."

I looked around my neighbor to see Fred's horseface molded in sanctity as he raised his beer, and Melva looking angelic on the next stool. He had a gentle smile on his lips, and Melva's green eyes were soft and demure. Immediately to her left, a middle-aged man stared through thick lenses at her. The bartender, arrested with a glass and bar towel in his hands, had a round face full of astonishment for Fred. He said nothing.

"Sister Bellows and I," Fred went on, indicating Melva, "strive to become as our fellow men on occasion and we wish to be one of the—uh, crowd. Regard us as ordinary customers, if you please. Another beer, if I may."

"Sure, Rever—"

Fred shut him off with a lean hand. "Not Reverend, please. I am Custer Bellows. Cuss, they called me in school." He peered at Melva's neighbor. "Brother, your mind is troubled. Perhaps Sister Bellows can give you a word of comfort."

"I should be most happy," Melva murmured, and turned the full brilliance of her eyes on the bespectacled man. "If you are in trouble, brother, allow me to advise you."

The middle-aged man put down his glass. "Ain't in no trouble," he muttered, and fled through the swinging doors.

Fred and Melva began to chuckle. "He had notions

about her," Fred explained to the bartender. "We've found a good way to get rid of such lugs."

"You almost had me tossin' in my towel," the bartender said. "You mean it was a gag?"

"Pure and simple."

"This one's on the house," the bartender said.

"That was the idea," Melva offered. She seemed to see me for the first time. "George! Come and split a beaker of brew."

The idea in my mind required privacy. I motioned them to a table. When we were seated, I said, "I have a job for both of you."

"If we have to go back to Hollywood," Melva said, "no soap. We're staying until you go."

I ignored her. I took a pencil and notebook, made a list of names. I gave them to Fred. "If necessary, hire a private inquiry agency. I want to know everything about those people, from birth till now. I want it arranged chronologically in separate reports. This is pretty vital. Both of you beat it."

"Every time we go away, you get in trouble," Melva objected. "I'm staying, to protect my meal ticket."

"Your meal ticket will do some punching of its own if you don't go," I told her. "I need the information as soon as possible. I have no need of you at all, here."

"Why is this so important?" Melva asked.

"Somebody on that list is Peggy's murderer. And somewhere in his past will be found the motive for killing Severance Flynne."

"You promised, George!"

"And I've broken my promise. I'm serious, Melva. Please get going."

She dropped her bantering attitude. "Certainly. If you're that serious, George. Well," she said to Fred, "harness the horses."

"Shall I bring this stuff back?" Fred asked.

"I'll be in Hollywood before you can finish." I wondered if this was true. Sheriff Callahan wasn't going to be happy about an unknown murderer leaving his bailiwick. I had a sudden vision of the whole company staying here indefinitely while the data on an unsolved crime gathered dust.

Lamar James returned late that afternoon. He came to my trailer. I had finished delivering Riegleman's suggestion to a select few, and was reading a copy of *Popular Mechanics*.

"Well," he said, "I got the dope on Flynne. Fat lot of good."

I fixed drinks. "Let's hear it."

He took out his notebook. "I had to do a flock of running around, and I talked to his mother on the telephone. But here it is. He was twenty-nine years old last March. He grew up on a farm, went to grade and high school, then to State College, studying scientific farming. Seems he wanted to be another Burbank. When he tried his newfangled theories, his old man raised hell, and Flynne left home. They didn't hear from him for about four years, except for postcards. These came from Chicago, New York, New Orleans, and finally Hollywood. I talked to a dozen people who knew him and they all turned in the same thing: he was a nice guy, he didn't run around with women, he didn't drink too much, but he spent lots of money on his friends. Nobody seemed to know where he got all the money, because he didn't work enough to earn it. He was behind in his board bill, too, but the landlady hadn't been worried. Every time he got a job, he paid up his bills. Between jobs, he just tossed parties for his friends. None of them knew that he had come up here till they read about it. Everybody was sorry, and nobody could think of any enemies he made."

He handed me his notebook. "Here's a list of all the people he knew from the time he was born, except for the few years he was away. I couldn't get a lead on that. It'd cost a lot, and I didn't know whether you wanted to spend it or not."

I ran over the list. "Where's Herman Smith? He was one of the persons you were particularly to see. I don't see a report of it."

"He's gone," James said. "Just disappeared into thin air. I couldn't find hide nor hair of him."

Chapter Twenty-Two

WHEN I REPORTED on location the next morning, I was tired. I had lain awake most of the night pondering the disappearance of Herman Smith and its possible significance. He was a direct contact, he could give us important information, and he was gone.

Paul had proposed a possible explanation of Flynne's death. If some person had deliberately aided Smith to get drunk the night before he was to leave for location, we could assume that that person was the murderer. Flynne was beyond questioning; we'd never know from him if he was tipped off to call Smith, or if Smith was tipped off to call him.

And now Smith was gone. Murdered? We had to find out. He was the critical factor now.

And so I was tired. I had a pair of Monday-morning eyes, red-rimmed, puffed, bloodshot. I was in no condition to argue with Wallingford or Riegleman.

They were deadlocked over the sandstorm. I had forgotten to mention it to Riegleman, and he reacted to Wallingford's suggestion with shocked disapproval while Sammy was quietly anxious, looking on.

It was Sammy's expression, I think, that brought

me into the fray. His round face was tight, his eyes both bitter and hopeful. He looked at me as if he were drowning and I was the man with the straw.

"Look at what it means," Wallingford said. "All the stuff we're trying to say it means. They fight through everything to give us Highway 101, and Sand Springs, and Hollywood and Vine. Nothing can stop 'em, not even trouble."

"I don't like it," Riegleman answered. "We have no script, for one thing, and I shudder to think of three hundred people ad libbing at once. We must find the author."

Sammy flung a plea at me. He said nothing, but his eyes spoke of McGuire and the missing gun.

"In the early days of pictures," I told Riegleman, "they made up the story as they went along. Surely we can film one scene that requires practically no dialogue. I agree with Wally. I think his idea is terrific."

Wallingford beamed at me, taking full credit for the idea. "They come to me, these things," he said.

Riegleman flung up his hands. "All right," he said. "It's your money. Let's get at it."

We worked out the details, with me doing most of the talking. Sammy went off to get the wind machines and cameras set up.

It was to be a short scene on the screen. We decided on a freak sandstorm that rose and died within a few moments. All we wanted to show was the steel determination of the pioneers, and their attitude during the storm would be as symbolic whether it lasted for minutes or days.

We decided also to push our actors through actual

blasts of sand instead of making a process shot. Since they were to be in it for fifteen minutes at most, no body would get hurt. Their defenses against it would be all the more realistic.

We were finally ready to begin, and my starting point was near the two stakes I had driven. The wind machines began to whip up a cloud on the big dune, and we began to stagger through it.

Carla and I were together. I had sent Frank to some other part of the caravan. Carla and I exchanged a significant glance, in close-up.

It was a tough scene, and I repented my bid for realism before I had gone fifteen steps into that opaque blast. I wrapped my nose and mouth with a bandanna, and shielded my eyes with my hand. I must arrive at the spot where Listless had thrown the guns within ten minutes.

But I began to be caught up in the historical significance of the scene. When the men and women we were portraying came to the far edge of the desert, they didn't know how far it extended. They could see only sand, sparse desert growth, and brown rocks pushing their naked heads against the tide of erosion that had leveled the land about them. Those men and women didn't know when, if ever, they would find water. They didn't know whether they would die and leave their bones to bleach with the skulls of cattle which were white warts on the desert's face. They went on with high courage.

I have been told that I was very good in the scene. If so, it was because of that sudden kinship with the man I represented. Hilary Weston had set himself a goal; I had set mine. His was to win through to life against odds. Mine was similar. Though he thought in terms of green valleys and fertile fields, and though I thought in terms of freedom from jail and appeasement of the property department, our aims were the same.

We fought that million-toothed wind for each inch we gained. We were not acting, we were struggling against the elements. Though they were man-made, they had the same effect on us as the blind forces of nature.

Carla and I became separated somehow, at about the point where I should begin my search. It was this accident which made my behavior a highlight of the picture.

I turned my back to the driving wind, and tried to locate the stakes, now far behind. I couldn't see twenty feet, of course, and a little panic struck me. Was I to fail, after this elaborate preparation? I stared wildly around, trying to find the big dune. I took quick, uncertain steps this way and that.

When this sequence showed on the screen, everyone who saw it knew that Hilary Weston, beset with death on all sides, threatened with painful extinction, still held the thought of Carla in his mind. Yes, he was bound to deliver his band, but he was also bound to have this beautiful girl.

As a matter of fact, any thought I gave to Carla was purely accidental. My stumbling this way and that was fright. I collected my emotions and stuffed them back where they belonged. I turned into the wind and pushed on.

This brought scattered handclaps later, at the preview. It was obvious that Hilary Weston, torn between the power of his desire and his unswerving purpose, decided to reach safety for the greatest number even if a few, Carla among them, were left behind.

I saw before me the dim, dark outline of the great dune. I skirted its base and stumbled forward to what I thought was the spot Sammy and I had searched yesterday. I staggered and fell to one knee, flinging up an arm to hide my searching eyes. I got up and fell forward again.

A dull gleam caught my eye, and I flung myself upon it. It was one of the guns. I lay quite still, my back to the camera, and felt in the sand. I found the other gun. I began a series of mighty heaves. I flung myself about, all the while stuffing the guns into my belt. I got to one knee, to my feet. I staggered on, straight at the lens, a gleam of unholy triumph in my eyes.

When all the stragglers were in, Curtis stepped up and shook my gritty hand. "If I know anything about how a scene will look on the screen," he said warmly, "you were magnificent. We got every move."

Sammy came over to whisper, "Did you get 'em?"

In my dressing room, Sammy looked at the Smith & Wesson while I made up for a retake of the fight scene.

"So this is it," he commented.

"Fully loaded," I pointed out, "except for one shot. That was the one which got Flynne, I believe."

"What do we do with it?"

"I'll turn it over to James in good time. Meanwhile, we flaunt it."

Sammy looked blank.

"I'll wear those two guns in this next scene. Since we're shooting it from the beginning, nobody will notice I've changed guns except the murderer. You can bet that he'll notice. As I have said before, he has an eye for detail. When he sees me with the gun, which he'll undoubtedly recognize, he'll be driven to action. I feel certain that he has worried about this gun. He planted it on me, and it disappeared. Nothing was said about it. He noted that I carried forty-fives yesterday. Now I show up with the murder weapon in my holster. Such procedure doesn't make sense. So he betrays himself, one way or another. I have told at least four persons to keep their eyes open during this scene. You must pay no attention to the action being filmed. Watch everyone behind the first camera. I think the murderer will make some covert move."

"You can't fire this gun, George. It's really loaded."

"Sammy," I said patiently, "go get me some blank cartridges. We'll save these, naturally, as evidence. Run along. I'm almost ready. And by the way," I added casually, "tell Paul I'd like to see him."

I waited by the first camera, the guns carelessly displayed. Nobody gave them a glance. The electricians were setting up reflectors, Curtis was measuring distances, Riegleman was conferring with the new script girl, sound men were testing with the boom crew. Horses were being led into the wagon enclosure.

Sammy and Paul returned, and I loaded the guns. Paul watched with disinterest.

"I want to apologize," I said, "for the heroic measures I employed last night."

"I'll never be able to wear a belt again," he growled, "and I hate suspenders. How come your guns don't match?"

I looked at him steadily. "One of them has a sentimental value," I said.

He blinked, shrugged, and turned away. As I had hoped, he lingered near the camera as I went off to my place.

Whistles called for quiet. Riegleman went into the sound truck and spoke over the P.A. system, his voice booming in precise syllables.

"This must be the last retake of this scene, ladies and gentlemen. It will be unnecessary to repeat my instructions. You know your parts. I am depending on you to play them well. Are we ready to begin?"

Sammy signaled, and action began.

I put the murders from my mind. Several pairs of eyes were examining all my list of suspects. I became Hilary Weston. I was careful, however, to display the murder weapon. I covered the butt of the museum piece with one hand, but turned the Smith & Wesson toward the camera as often as possible. Even if this did not bring any untoward act from Paul, it might when tomorrow's rushes showed it in close-up.

Halfway through the scene, I reflected that he must still have the gun that killed Peggy. Would he take a shot when I faced the camera today? It was possible. He had noted the gun and commented. He was ruthless, and I was defenseless.

I must confess that cold sweat trickled down my back as I turned for the close-up of passion. This was the point where two persons had been killed. Was I next?

The beads of sweat on my forehead were real. The trembling of my hands was not pantomime. Only a few seconds remained in the scene, and I did what has been called one of my finest bits of acting, but I wish to record here that I was not acting. I was not even aware that I was in a picture. When I looked at the camera, it was desperation, not lust, that the camera recorded. Yes, it seemed lustful on the screen. It was obvious that even in the midst of battle I was savoring secret delights to come. And when I narrowed my eyes and pointed the gun at the group beside the camera, it was not thoughts of a sneaking redskin that inspired me.

For Paul was in that group, and one dark hand was in his jacket pocket. My aiming at him was a reflex action, and I wished with all my heart that my gun was loaded as I fired at him.

My expression and action brought a gasp to the preview audience several weeks later, as did the quick cut to a tomahawked figure that had sneaked within striking distance of Carla. But he was an afterthought, tossed in to explain my unscripted move. All I was trying to do was startle Paul, to shake his aim, to make him miss.

The result was rather spectacular. Everyone in the

group flung himself to this side or that. Some fell flat on the ground, others jerked spasmodically to one side. Paul flung both hands, empty, over his face. My danger was passed, and the smile of relief which I gave the lens was properly construed at the preview, indicated by the audience's vast, soft sigh.

When whistles brought a halt, they crowded around me, flinging praise.

"George, you were swell!"

". . . finest piece of . . ."

"Didn't know pantomime was one of your . . ."

"Worth ten thousand words of dialogue!"

Riegleman hurried from the sound truck, from which he had watched and listened to the scene, and put an arm across my shoulders. "George, old boy, you'll get an award for that scene. I'll give it to you myself if the Academy doesn't."

Hands grasped at mine, hands slapped my shoulders. I was a trifle bewildered. I hadn't done anything but protect my life.

"But what I want to know," Riegleman went on, "is why you fired that shot. It wasn't in the script, as I remember, and you played the scene day before yesterday with your guns at your sides."

That was when I dreamed up the sneaking tomahawker. Riegleman glowed. "A wonderful touch. Let's shoot it." He beckoned to one of the Indians and Curtis. They went off to make it.

The crowd dissolved from around me. Sammy took my arm. "I thought sure as hell I was a goner," he said. "You should have seen your face. I just *knew* that gun was loaded."

"Did you observe anything?" I asked.

"Let's go talk it over," Sammy said. "Maybe you can make something of what I saw. Want me to put those guns away?"

I reached for them. My left hand closed on an empty holster. Somebody had taken the Smith & Wesson from me.

Chapter Twenty-Three

"GO TO YOUR OFFICE!" I said. "I'll see you there in a few minutes!"

"What's the matter with you? You look like a label on a carbolic acid bottle."

"I'm tired of being pushed around," I said, and plunged off through the sand.

Paul was alone in his office. He narrowed his eyes at my expression. His hands tensed on his desk.

"Where is it?" I asked.

"Where is what?"

"The gun you took out of my holster. I'm going to take this office, and you, apart if you don't give it to me."

He leaned back, his mouth dropped open. "Come again?"

"I don't want to argue," I told him. "Just give me the gun, and you may remain intact. You *may*. It isn't definite."

"I don't know what you're talking about, George. I know you're serious. But you're talking acrostics."

I took the slack of his shirt in one hand and pulled him to his feet. "I don't really want to hurt you, Paul, but I'll make you an unpleasant memory if you don't hurry."

He didn't struggle. His black eyes weren't defiant, they were bewildered. "I can't stop you, I guess, George. You're almost twice my size, and I'm in lousy shape. But, honest to God, I don't know what you're talking about."

He seemed to be telling the truth. A little doubt raised its head inside mine. My grip relaxed for an instant, and he jerked away. I leaped after him, crowded him into a corner.

"You confessed to the killing," I said. "But you deliberately tried to make me believe that you lied. I did, and dismissed you from consideration. But here's what you did. You shot Flynne. You switched guns on me. You planted that prop gun in Carla's wagon. You pleaded ignorance of Flynne's identity. You came to my trailer that night to find out if the film showed anything damaging to you. Then you shot Peggy with your other gun, because you knew she had seen you. Then you made a confession, with false data, to throw me off. But I see through it now. So where are the guns?"

His black eyes began to water. He made no effort to defend himself. "I didn't . . . kill anybody!" he gasped. "I thought . . . Carla would be accused. I don't know . . . anything about a gun. But listen, I've . . . got an idea."

I dropped my hands, but kept him in the corner.

"It just occurred to me," he said. "Herman Smith was leading a double life, sort of. I got a notion that fits into this picture."

"What does 'sort of' mean?"

"Listen, George," he said earnestly. "It's hard to say exactly what I mean. I can see how you'd jump to the conclusion you reached, but you're wrong. You can go ahead and search this place if you want to. If I took a gun from you, I haven't had time to do anything with it. It has to be here. It isn't. I'll help you search."

He meant it, which in turn meant that the gun wasn't here. He interpreted my half smile correctly.

"I insist," he said. "I've got to clear myself on that score. I didn't kill anybody, and this will help prove it."

We went over every inch of the office—including the wastebasket, this time. There wasn't any gun.

"You could have tossed it into one of the trucks," I said.

"So could anybody else. If it turns up in one of them, it doesn't necessarily mean that I did it. You've got no proof, George, that I'm involved in any way. So you've got to string along with me. I've got an idea."

"Let's hear it."

"No, because it's dopey. It'll just lead you off the track if it doesn't work out. I'll find out today, and come over to your trailer tonight."

I felt sick. As he said, I could do nothing. My notions were based on deduction and application of psychology. I couldn't go to Sheriff Callahan with them. "Look, Sheriff, I have no proof at all, but he did it. I feel it here. I can't find any motive, and I can't prove that he had the opportunity. But I'm sure, so will you charge him with murder on my hunch?"

Callahan, even Callahan, would snort at me.

"Give me some idea of what you're going to do," I said.

"It all depends," he said, "on who Herman Smith really is. I heard a rumor once. I want to check it. If it's true, you can find a motive, all right."

"What was the rumor?"

"I haven't even got that straight. I have to check with a couple guys in Hollywood. Then I'll tell you tonight."

What could I do? I did it. "All right, but God help you if this another lie. Paul, you're in this up to your neck. I can have you held for questioning, if nothing else. Maybe you'd better tell me some more about Carla and Flynne before I go."

"Not unless I have to," he said. "There's no reason why it should come out except to free her from suspicion. She's got a great future. If it all came out, she'd be hurt commercially."

"If you're going to marry her, you don't want her earning ability impaired. Is that it?"

He grinned frankly. "Something like that." He looked at me in sudden alarm. "Stop getting purple, George! I really love the gal. I think she's wonderful."

I had to shrug, finally. It wasn't the first time some girl was married for the money she was able to make. And that was none of my business.

"By the way," he said conversationally. "It seems to me that you're on something of a spot. You say you had the murder weapon. You played this last scene with it. If you can't dig up proof that somebody planted it on you, it's going to look bad, eh?"

It wasn't an open threat, but his shrewd eyes carried all the implications. I said nothing. After a long stare, I went away.

Sammy had his head in his hands. He looked up as I came in. "Well, anyway, you've still got the museum piece, George. Now we got to get the other from that deputy."

"I'll do that today."

I sat down. We didn't say anything. There was nothing to say. All paths of investigation seemed to be closed to me. If I had hung on to the gun, or if I had seen who took it from me, the problem would have been solved. Certain routine matters could have rolled into operation. We could have checked the serial number, and sweated out the truth from the man who had the gun in his possession. After all, if I had seen who took it, I'd have seen the murderer.

I was out of my depth, and I knew it. It was a sad admission. I had felt confident all along. It would be only a matter of hours before I could point a melodramatic finger and say, *"Ecce homo!"* At one time, I had had all the factors fairly clear in my mind. One of a certain group was the murderer. The actions of a few of that group had attracted my attention, which grew to suspicion and dissipated into nothingness. I had wound up with no definite suspect, with nothing but the knowledge of unrelated acts, and without the gun.

I got to my feet and went out, saying nothing to Sammy. I don't believe that he noticed my going.

Lamar James was in his laboratory. He was tipped back in a chair, his feet on a table with two microscopes, his eyes on far space. He grinned mildly at me.

"I'm trying to work out a mathematical equation, George. But I've been trying for two years. What's on your mind?"

"I need help."

I sat down. He took a bottle of chemical analysis alcohol from a cupboard, put a teaspoonful in each of two glasses, filled them with water, and gave me one. It tasted something like good gin, and warmed a path down my gullet.

"When Flynne was killed," I began, "I had a pair of valuable guns in my hands. They were Colt thirty-eights on forty-five frames, pearl handled." His dark eyes sparked. He flicked a glance at another cupboard. "During the crush after the scene," I went on, "somebody took one of those guns. He replaced it with what I believe to be the gun that killed Flynne. Sammy took both guns from me, and noticed the strange weapon. He decided to put them in his office, and ask me about it later. His girl friend, who knew he was worried about them, threw both guns on the other side of a big sand dune when she heard somebody had been shot. We couldn't find them, and then you turned up one of the original pair in Carla's wagon."

"You knew it was there," James broke in. "When you got that blanket to cover Flynne, you saw it. I figured that out later. You should have told me then."

"But look at my position. The sheriff is inclined to go off half-cocked. He could have arrested me."

"I could pinch you now for obstructing justice."

"Wait until I finish," I said. "You'll do whatever seems best then."

I told him of the parade of people who came to my trailer that night, and related their conversations. He listened without interruption.

"I was ready to give up and tell you what I knew," I said. "I knew that if I made that scene over, carrying forty-fives, Peggy would notice. Then she was killed. I lost my head, I suppose. It became a personal matter. Flynne hadn't meant anything to me. My going into the investigation was strictly a move of self-defense. But when Peggy got a slug in the back, I was furious. Revenge was what I wanted. Personal revenge. And I knew more of the currents than you. I figured I could work alone better than with you. There was still the matter of the missing gun, too."

I told him about Paul, and my conclusions. I told him Paul was coming to my trailer.

James thought silently for a long time. Finally he said, "I'll come over and listen to what he has to say. But I'll tell you this much, George. You're not in the clear. I haven't seen any proof of your innocence. The film is missing. And you could have shot the Whittier girl. You say she threw up a hand as if to stop everything, and then fell over. I don't see how you can prove that she didn't turn around to tell somebody behind her, Riegleman, for instance, and you let her have it."

"But I was carrying forty-fives then. I can prove that."

"But can you prove that you didn't also have a Smith & Wesson thirty-eight special on you?"

"I wouldn't have dared, with the camera on me in a close-up."

"I saw the—whatcha call 'em? Rushes? The critical shot of you was a close-up, showing only your head and shoulders. Who knows what you did with your hands?"

"You're joking!"

"Not more than half," he countered. "I've got to regard you as a suspect. Look at how it stacks up. You took that reel of film, which you claim would show you to be innocent. It disappeared while in your possession. You *could* have wanted to destroy it."

"Look," I said, "I came in here of my own free will trying to clarify this thing. Now we're off on another tangent. I didn't kill Flynne. I'd never even seen him before."

"That's what everybody says," James went on patiently. "Somebody's lying. So I can't believe anybody."

"I have some corroboration. Sammy and Miss Nelson."

"What can they testify? One that you had the gun, the other that she threw it away. Does that prove anything?"

"What are you going to do about it?"

"Nothing—yet. I have a couple of ideas. I'm letting them ride."

"If I'm not under arrest, then, I'm going to eat."

"Go ahead. I'll see you at your trailer."

I went to the restaurant in the hotel. Wallingford, Riegleman, Paul, and Sammy were together at a table. I joined them.

"Sunsets are corny," Wallingford was saying. "The scene would be better in a dark cellar. It would mean something, too."

"I don't give a damn about the sunset," Riegleman said, wearily. "All I want is *something*. I've spent more than sixty dollars in telephone calls trying to find Connaught. We can't have any scene until we locate him."

Wallingford made a sudden decision. "Everybody get packed. We'll leave tomorrow morning. We got all we need here, and if I say so myself it's terrific."

"I think I'll drive down tonight," I said. "I have an appointment in an hour." I looked at Paul, who nodded imperceptibly. "After I keep it, I'm free."

I went out to my trailer, to find James waiting. I explained my electric-eye apparatus for turning on the lights, which brought up the subject of my telephone apparatus. I told him what I was trying to do.

"You've got it now so that you can take incoming calls?" he asked.

"Yes, but I have to open the base of the phone to hang up. I'll be glad to be back. I'm going to whip that little problem."

James looked impatiently at his watch. "Where's Paul?"

"He'll be along any time now."

We heard a flat *spat* outside, apparently originating

a considerable distance away. It could have been a backfire on the highway. We sat tensely.

"That was a shot," James said. "Let's take a look."

We went outside. We were blind in the sudden darkness, but scattered stars shed a kind of light when our eyes became adjusted. The stars were only a random handful of gems flung on velvet, but they showed a dark bundle some twenty feet away.

The bundle was Paul. He was dead, shot in the back.

"Then he was telling me the truth," I said slowly. "I'm sorry I acted the way I did."

We were in James's car, with Paul in the back seat. We roared into town behind the siren. We slid under the porte-cochere of a private hospital, and attendants carried Paul inside. James and I waited while the doctor extracted the bullet.

Presently it was delivered to him, and we went to his laboratory. He made a brief examination under the comparison microscope, then looked at me.

"Well," he said. "This came out of the same gun that killed Flynne. The one you say was stolen from you today."

"The one I *say* was stolen," I said. "Look, James, even you'll have to admit I was with you when that gun was used on Paul, or should I try to get a few witnesses?"

James nodded. "Don't bother with the witnesses, George. I guess this lets you out."

I tried not to sound as relieved as I felt. "Then I'll be on my way. It's your party from now on. I've messed around in it too much already. I guess I wasn't cut out to be a detective," I admitted handsomely.

"I'm afraid you'd better stick around," he said. "These murders occurred in our county. We can't let anybody get into another county until we've tabbed the killer."

"You can't hold the whole company here!"

"Can't we?" he asked grimly. "You just watch."

Chapter Twenty-Four

ONE REASON why Wallingford was popular was that he would fight for his own. On this occasion he was fighting for his shooting schedule, but he had fought as fiercely before for one of his people. Many times. There was the occasion when a prominent comedian hit the headlines with a slosh and studio moguls cancelled his contracts. Wallingford had stormed into the executive vice-president's office, like a circus performer striding into the lion's cage.

"Where do headlines wind up?" he'd yelled. "In a morgue! But pictures go to the Museum of Modern Art! Is a bottle as big as immortality? I'm gonna gnaw the bars outa that jail, and he's gonna finish my picture, even if it costs you a hundred grand! Besides, he's a good guy. Anybody can take a quart too many sometimes. Besides, people that live on glass bottles shouldn't throw stones! That's my final word!"

On the morning after Paul's death, he fixed Sheriff Call-Me-Jerry Callahan with a Damascene stare.

"Are you gonna arrest us all? You're gonna feed us, too? Listen, Mr. Sheriff, we got investments in this company. It's gonna cost somebody money to hold us up, and it ain't going to be me. That's my final word!"

"Now, Mr. Wallingford," Callahan said soothingly, "look at where I set. One of you is a murderer, and I got jurisdiction here. I got to catch you, whoever he is."

"Stop looking at me like a bail bond!" Wallingford snapped. "I wasn't even here when that extra got it!"

"But I can't take a chance," Callahan went on. "All I know is, somebody in your crowd done it. I expect to make an arrest at any moment."

"How?" Wallingford demanded. "George don't know, and he's smart. You got a crystal ball and chain somewhere?"

"We have our methods," Callahan said uneasily.

"You give me an ear for a minute," Wallingford said. "This is the fifth day since we got up here. We had a murder each on the first two days. And now last night. And I ain't observed you do nothing but sit on your backside. You think you're gonna wait till the murderer dies of hard arteries and makes a deathbed confession? Mister, time is money to us. I personally will go to the voters and tell 'em what you've done. I personally will see that hotel clerk's grandson made sheriff."

"He ain't old enough," Callahan said in mild triumph.

"We'll age him! We'll let him read your record in office. That would give a billiard ball gray hair."

"You gotta stay," the sheriff said doggedly.

I cut in, in the interests of Wallingford's apoplexy. "Just a moment, gentlemen. Let me show you something."

I gave Callahan a telegram which had arrived that morning. He read it, frowned at me, read it again.

"Ain't Paul Revere dead?" he demanded belligerently.

"You can't claim any of us did *that*," Wallingford said quickly.

"The signature," I said, "is my press agent's quaint idea of a gag. But that telegram gives us a clue. It says that the core of our problem is in Hollywood. We'll never—"

"It don't say nothing of the kind," Callahan interrupted. "It says—" He peered at the message. "It says 'THE BRITISH ARE COMING SIGNED PAUL REVERE.' Wasn't there something about a lantern in that story?"

"One if by land, and two if by sea," I said. "But what I started to—"

"My little niece," Wallingford put in, "knows it by heart. Five years old, she says, 'Listen, my chillun' —she don't talk so plain, but she talks—'and you can hear' and however it goes from there."

"That's pretty poetry," Sheriff Callahan said. "Don't see how them guys think up all them rhymes. Can't do it myself. Tried once, but couldn't find nothing to rhyme with revolver. I got it right here somewheres." He began to rummage in his desk. "Maybe you could help me with it, Mr. Sanders. You use big words."

I gritted my teeth. I said, without opening them, "I'd be glad to, Sheriff."

He handed me a sheet of paper, blank except for one scrawled line:

The Malibu Kid pulled out his revolver.

"Got stuck there," he said. "Think it's any good so far?"

"It has action," I said. "The story line isn't any too clear. Suppose he's going to shoot the girl who double-crossed him. It could go something like this:

"The Malibu Kid pulled out his revolver,

And aimed it at Calico Lee.

He called for the priest to come and absolve her.

He despised double-crossers, did he.

"You could go on and tell how she talked him out of it, and let them go into a tear-jerking clinch at the last."

"Say!" Callahan exclaimed. "That's swell. Here, lemme just write that out. I'll show my old lady, in my own handwritin'."

We waited until the scratch of his pencil ceased. He looked at me amiably. "Sure do thank you, Mr. Sanders. Now what was it you was sayin'?"

"I said that we'll never find the murderer here. We'll find him in Hollywood."

"But he ain't *in* Hollywood, he's here. And if he ever gets to Hollywood, we'll lose him. My brother-in-law's nephew—nice young fella with a wife and kids—went into a bar on Wilcox Street five years ago, and nobody seen him since."

"That," I said patiently, "isn't what I mean, Sheriff.

The motive can be found in Hollywood. All we need is the motive. It will point to the killer."

"But if I let three hundred people loose in Hollywood, the voters is gonna be sore."

"Send along your deputy. All of our names and addresses are on record. If any one of us skips, it will be easy to catch him. And James would be on hand to make the arrest."

"We got no allotment to take care of deputies' travel expenses."

"Oh, we'll pay his expenses," I said impatiently.

"Now, that's different," Callahan replied. "How much? He's got to have at least twelve-fifty a day."

"That's what we pay a good extra!" Wallingford cried. "He can't act, can he? Seven-fifty is all we pay, and he buys his own gas!"

"Then you stay here," Callahan pronounced. "Twelve-fifty or no go."

"But he ain't worth twelve-fifty, Sheriff. He'd be a dead loss, and if we gotta lose, we can't lose no more than seven-fifty."

"Wadda you care?" Callahan yelled. "You got lots of money!"

"I didn't get it by giving deputy sheriffs joy rides," Wallingford said stubbornly.

"It will be only a few days, Wally," I said.

"I don't care if it's a few hours, George. It ain't the principle of the thing, it's the money. It didn't used to cost so much to buy a cop, and the cops ain't any better today, even with the price of living going up. It's too expensive. Seven-fifty, that's my final word."

"How about ten dollars?" Callahan proposed. "And a bonus for me if I get him inside a week?"

"Eight," Wallingford countered.

Callahan pondered. "Nope," he said finally. "Nine-fifty's my lowest figger."

"Eight-twenty-five."

"Nine-twenty-five."

"Eight-thirty-three," Wallingford said.

"Nine dollars." The sheriff was getting desperate.

"I'm losing money," Wallingford said sadly, "but eight-fifty."

"Aw, come on, Mr. Wallingford. Have a heart. I'll settle for eight-seventy-five. I *can't* come no lower!"

Wallingford was adamant. "Eight-sixty-six. That's my final offer."

"I won't take it. I just won't."

"And two-thirds!" Wallingford spat.

Sheriff Callahan grinned. "Guess that's the best I can get. I'll take it." He chuckled. "Woulda settled for six bucks. Guess I got the best of ya."

"Ha!" Wallingford snapped. "I would've paid fifty."

Nine-thirty a.m. Perhaps Carla wasn't up yet. Somebody had to tell her, and now was a good time, while the bargain hunters settled details in the sheriff's office.

I went to the hotel, where a quartet of Los Angeles reporters leaped at me.

"How's it going, George?"

"Catch him yet?"

"Give us something for your fans. You should see the mail, since we announced that you were going to solve it!"

"You've got the female vote, George. And a whole gallery of pictures."

I waved them back. "There are no new developments," I said formally. "A startling announcement is expected momentarily."

"Oh, come, George. Give us something. The city desk will chew my ears if I don't turn in something."

"All right, boys. Since my press agent put me out on a limb, I may as well go all the way. You can say this. The same person killed all three victims."

They yawned.

"What can I say?" I asked reasonably. "We haven't caught the killer. We may or may not catch him. There you have the truth."

"You can't expect us to print that, George."

"Why not? The truth would be a novelty to your readers."

"Look, Sanders, we're not concerned very much over how you do on this. We're giving you a chance to appear in a good light. The announcement of your entrance into the case as a sleuth caused a mild sensation. You're on a spot with your public. If you don't deliver, you'll lose popularity. If you'll be nice to us, we'll gloss over your failure, if you fail. But if you're not, we can sure as hell kill you off with hardening of the adjectives."

There was truth, all right. It raised right up and took a sock at my bank roll.

"Fail?" I said coldly. "I won't fail. I have no information for you except the usual junk about an early arrest. But if you insist, I'll give you a prediction. I'll have the killer nailed to a warrant day after tomorrow."

"That's professional suicide, George! You don't dare, unless you have a lot of dope you haven't told us. It's just suicide!"

"I was driven to it," I said grimly. "I have a hunch, and I'm playing it. So far I've just been playing Now I'm playing a hunch."

"Well, if you want to take that chance, we'll headline it. Let the contracts fall where they may."

"The Sanders luck will bring me through," I said. "The company is leaving now, boys. We are to be accompanied by the deputy sheriff. I suppose you can call it technical arrest. You can make something of that."

"Where do we find this deputy?"

I told them. They flocked to the door. "We'll go as easy as possible, George," one called back.

"Is Miss Folsom in?" I asked Lazarus Fortescue.

"You want to know something?" he asked. "I set here an' I look. I see lots of people, over ten years. All kinds. But I ain't never seen any dopier people than you guys. Where's all this wild Hollywood carryin' on?"

"We've had three murders."

"Ain't what I mean. That could happen to ladies' sewin' circle. Good thing, too. What I mean is everbody got a room to hisself an' stays in it. An' when you go up to see one o' those babes, you just talk. Tommy told me. He listened."

"Is he studying to be a press agent?"

"Nope. He just listens 'cause he knows he'll get the hell whaled out of him if he gets caught. He sure got hell yestiddy, from me. I spanked him, an' he can't come here for a week. Don't hold with stealin'. Listenin's fun, but stealin's means spankin's. Even if it was just an old flat tin can, he had no call to take it."

It was probably only thirty seconds before I could trust myself to speak, but it seemed like thirty years. I said very casually, "Odd thing to steal. Where is it, do you know? I'd like to see it."

"Oh, I got it here. Figgered somebody would ask."

He put it on the desk. It was the missing reel, unharmed.

"Where did he get this?"

"He says he don't remember. I told him to take it back, an' he says he can't think which room it was. I whaled him, an' he still wouldn't tell. I don't think you could make him tell now. Stubborn as a mule."

"This is vitally important," I said. "Please bring him here and let me talk to him."

"If you just stick your head out the door, guess you'll see him hangin' around till I let him in."

Tommy was there. He came in reluctantly, and made a face at his grandfather. "I hate you!" he said.

"Now, Tommy, I'll smack you."

"I don't care," Tommy growled, "I hate you anyway."

I broke into this domestic scene. "Tommy, you took that tin can from a room. I want you to show me which room."

He scowled at me. "Been whipped already."

"Nobody will whip you, Tommy. I'll even give you a dollar if you'll show me."

"Don't want a dollar, want a quarter."

"If I give you a quarter, will you show me?"

He eyed me craftily. "Maybe."

"What do you mean, maybe?"

"Ain't got the quarter yet."

I gave him a quarter. He bit it, tucked it into his pocket. "When I show you, gimme another one?"

"Yes, I'll give you another."

"Less see it," he demanded.

"What do you do," I asked his grandfather, "lie to him constantly? I never saw such a suspicious child."

"His ma told him 'twouldn't hurt when th' doctor set his leg. Shouldn'ta lied to him. Can't blame the kid."

"Well, here's the other quarter, Tommy. It's yours when you tell me where you got the can."

I tucked the film under my arm and followed him. He led me to Wanda's door. "It was in the waste-basket," he whispered. "I didn't think it was stealin'. Gimme my quarter."

I gave it to him, and he ran downstairs.

Carla finished her make-up after she admitted me, and I watched her mirrored reflection. She didn't know about Paul. That was obvious. Her dark eyes were merry, her skin clear and milky.

"So we're going home," she said.

"Yes, and I came to offer you a ride."

Her eyes sparkled at me in the mirror. "Thanks, but I have a ride."

"Carla, I have something to tell you. You won't like it. Paul is dead."

She caught her breath. All color drained from her face. She fixed her eyes on mine in the mirror. She didn't move for a long time. Finally, she whispered, "When?"

"Last night, about eight o'clock."

She seemed to relax a little. "How?"

"He was shot by the same gun that killed Flynne."

She whirled on me. "No!" she gasped. "That's too much. That's just too much!"

"Aren't you taking the death of your fiance pretty casually?"

"How did you know?" she demanded. "He told you, I suppose. He wasn't taking any chances. Yes, I'm taking it casually."

"Maybe you'd better tell me the whole story now. Or would you rather tell it to the police?"

Her mouth twisted with bitterness. "I guess I have to tell you. I had to tell Paul. I hope you don't pull the same trick."

I waited a long time before she spoke again.

"I told you I was a little girl from Brooklyn, George. When I was almost sixteen, I met Sev Flynne. I'd never met anybody like him before, so full of dreams, so gentle and ambitious at the same time. We fell in love, and we got tired of whispering on bus tops and in hallways. We wanted to get married. But I was under age, and I knew my family would never consent. But he explained to me that marriage was never any more than a contract between two people and God. He made it sound very beautiful. I agreed to do what he wanted."

She paused to twist a little smile. She was lovely. "We went out on a ferry boat," she went on, "and climbed up on the top deck. There we made our solemn vows. 'I, Severance, take thee, Mildred'—that was my name— 'to be my lawful' and so on. It was wonderful. And all the new experiences were wonderful, too. We had enough money to rent a hall bedroom, and lost ourselves in New York. I changed my name then, because I knew my family would be looking for me. I got in touch with them, three years later. May I have a cigarette?"

I lighted two, gave her one. She nodded, and went on, "He wanted to be an engineer, and was working out his tuition in school. I went to work, and we lived on my sixteen dollars a week. I was a housewife—I was a *wife*, a woman—and I cried, I was so happy, at times. I worshiped him, and he seemed to worship me.

"One day he came home and said he wasn't going back. He had flunked a test, and there wasn't, he said, much future in engineering. The future was in aviation. He went out to a field and washed airplanes for flying lessons. He was going to be a great pilot, and he read all the flying stories he could get. He wrote a poem once, called it *Song of the Ace*, and it was printed in an aviation magazine. They gave him a three-month subscription for his poem." She paused, then said reflectively, "It wasn't a very good poem."

I said, "And then?"

"Then he was suddenly afraid to get off the ground. I don't know what happened, but he lost his nerve. He wouldn't even talk about it. He was going to work in a bank. That was a safe business. But he couldn't get a job, and he started selling vacuum cleaners door to door. He was going to be a salesman whose record would go down in history.

"Well, he couldn't sell, and by this time—nearly four years later—I was sick of my bargain. I guess I still loved him, in a way, but we began to fight. He accused me of thinking he was no good, but he'd show me, just wait. It went on hour after hour until I could scream.

"About that time, Gary Blake stopped me on the street, and I told you about that. Well, right after I got my first important role, I got a letter from Sev. He said he understood, and he had no claim on me. Any time two people couldn't stay together peaceably, they ought to separate, he said. And he had been thinking that he was really cut out to be an actor. He was coming to Hollywood, and he'd show them what acting really was. Could I send him the fare?"

She looked at me, a kind of tender sadness in her eyes. "I knew what that meant, and I couldn't get out of it. It meant that I was to support him the rest of his life. I sent him the fare, and 'loaned' him money regularly. He told me once that he lived on money that he earned. He was too proud to let me support him. He was investing the money that I gave him, he said."

I thought of Lamar James' report. Flynne "invested" that money in parties for his friends.

"Well," she said, "I was in a funny position. We had lived together under common law long enough to be legally man and wife, but if the circumstances were known, it wouldn't do me any good. It would do me a great deal of harm.

"Now comes the clincher.

"Paul had talked to me several times. Once he threw a good role my way. Later, he ran into Sev. Sev got drunk with him and told Paul about me. So Paul blackmailed me into promising to marry him, and we let a few intimate friends in on the secret. But I couldn't get a divorce from a man I'd never really married. It seems silly, but that's the way it was. That's why I was so frightened when I found that Sev had got into this picture somehow, and had been killed. He was the only person standing between Paul and me getting married, and when that gun was found in my wagon—"

"Didn't you suspect Paul?"

"No. Paul wasn't a killer. He didn't have the nerve. I didn't suspect anybody. All I knew was that *I* was the perfect suspect, with motive and everything."

I provided fresh cigarettes. Was this truth? It could be, but on the other hand, she was capable of dreaming up this yarn. Much as I wanted to believe it, I couldn't accept it unequivocally. She had been frightened when I told her Paul was dead.

"Why were you so scared when I told you about Paul?" I asked. "Why did you ask 'When?' "

"Because I was in the restaurant from seven until nine. I was downstairs having dinner, and can prove it. My first thought was that somebody knew about the three of us, and was trying to put the killings onto me. I had motive, you must admit. But to have both Sev and Paul killed by the same gun—well, I couldn't believe it. *Why* were they?"

"I just assume that was the murderer's favorite shooting iron," I said. "Do you want to ride with me back to Hollywood?"

"I guess so," she said heavily. "If somebody doesn't knock you off before we start. I seem to be bad luck."

Chapter Twenty-Five

A s we passed through hills to the north of Santa Barbara, with the sea veiled in fog on our right, I said, "You're right, Carla; your story makes you the only one so far with motive."

She didn't turn her head. "I've been thinking about that," she replied, in little more than a whisper. "But I wouldn't have killed either of them. I didn't mind giving Sev money. I got into the habit when we were married. And as for Paul, even though I resented his methods, I think he forced me into the position he did because he honestly loved me and saw no other way. I didn't especially want to marry him—if and when I could—but I didn't especially *not* want to, either."

"Assuming that you're telling the truth—"

She turned her head on this. "Assuming?" she asked sharply. "Don't you believe me?"

"I want to. But how can I? I don't know you very well. We aren't, and never have been, really intimate friends. How do I know what your private life is like? By your own admission, you fit the part completely. You had motive, and there is no evidence that you didn't have the means and opportunity. You were only a few feet from where Flynne was shot, and you were out of camera range."

"And Peggy?" she asked. "Are you trying to say that I shot Peggy in the back?"

"I was about half accused of doing it," I said. "If I could have done it, you could."

"Well, then, how about Paul? Whoever shot him must have shot Sev. And I can prove I didn't shoot Paul."

"Yes, that's true," I said morosely.

"You needn't sound as if you're sorry it wasn't I!"

"I haven't ever thought it was you. I'm eliminating now. Tell me something. You had a close-up immediately after I did when Flynne was shot. Try to recall everything you saw when you faced the camera."

She was quiet through a long lane of eucalyptus. I stuck my head out for a periodic look at my trailer. She stuck a lighted cigarette in my mouth and stared moodily at oncoming traffic. The cigarette smoke mingled pleasantly with the smell of eucalyptus.

"I saw Mr. Curtis, first of all," she said at last. "I was supposed to look at him. Then the man who was actually shooting the scene, and Peggy, and Riegleman standing behind her. Then a couple of electricians—Joe and Charley, their names are—and the men operating the boom. And Sammy, of course. I could see one of the sound men inside the sound wagon. I guess that's about all."

"Behind them?" I prodded. "Think hard."

"Even if I had seen anyone," she said, "I probably wouldn't have noticed. You know the mood I was

in. I was supposed to be looking at you. I seem to
have seen that little blonde girl in wardrobe. I'm not
sure."

"Did you notice what any of them were doing?"

"No. I didn't care."

"I'm sure," I said more to myself than to her, "that
you have named the murderer. One of those people
did the killings."

"But why? Sev didn't even know them. I know he
didn't. He tore around with a different crowd. Aside
from Paul, he didn't know anybody in this company
—except maybe for a few extras. And you can't put
the killing on Paul."

I waited for a break so that I could pass an oil
truck before I spoke. When I was halfway around,
I saw that I was in for a tight squeeze with a big car
roaring toward me. The truck driver, with the cour-
tesy of his kind, slowed and slid over to give me
room. I honked my thanks and went on.

"Let's take them in order," I said. "You mentioned
Curtis. He seems like a nice little fellow to me. I
should imagine that we can eliminate him from the
suspect list. Still, he doesn't follow any set pattern of
movement. Nobody would notice if he stepped aside
and took a shot at somebody."

"But Sev didn't know him! I'm sure of that."

"It's a cinch he knew somebody," I said impatiently. "I'm trying to find out whom."

"He didn't, though. But go on."

"Well, there was Riegleman. He's free to move
around too. He'd have even more opportunity than
Curtis. Are you sure Flynne didn't know him?"

"Of course I'm sure. Look, George. Here's something I haven't told you. Sev came to my room the night we arrived. He wanted to apologize for taking this job. He said he didn't know that I was on the picture or he wouldn't have done it. He also told me that he didn't know anybody. He'd talked to Wanda on the train, but it was just chit-chat. So we figured there wasn't any danger in appearing together on the set. He was always over-meticulous about the situation, aside from that time he got drunk with Paul. He went to fantastic lengths not to be identified with me in any way."

"Then that gives us no motive for Riegleman, and whoever killed him had the strongest of motives. Hell," I said in disgust, "it gives us no motive for anybody. Unless it was the Nelson girl, and he didn't tell you he knew her."

"The what girl?"

"The blonde in wardrobe."

I thought about this for a while. Suppose Listless had the motive, and suppose that she could shoot. She had the means and opportunity, then. Would she have acted subsequently in the way she did? Perhaps. She would have made an attempt to get rid of the murder weapon, but—

No, she wouldn't have told us where she threw it. She could have misdirected us by twenty feet, and we'd never have found it.

What, I asked myself, did all this have to do with the identity of Herman Smith? Paul had said he'd heard a rumor, and after he'd checked it, he was going to let me know. What could that mean?

And did Fred's insane telegram mean anything except that he was riding here and there, trying to get information?

I gave it up. For the rest of the trip, we talked about the picture and the faults of other actors.

I looked at the reports in Melva's office. "So these are they," I said.

"Yes, them's them. Listen, George, I have always regarded you as being normally bright. Until today. What are you trying to do, make yourself a laughing stock? You can't afford to make people laugh at you unless they pay at the box office. Free laughs will kill you off."

I looked up from the report on Charley, the electrician. "Riddles, dear?"

"Day after tomorrow, indeed! Who do you think you are, Ellery Queen?"

"Ellery Queen is a myth."

"Stop lisping! He's a mister. He's a detective. Can you say as much?"

"I can qualify in certain respects. I'm in a hurry, pet. Where's Fred, and why aren't all the reports here?"

"He's out getting the rest. He said for you to look at this clipping. He said you'd know why."

She showed me a society page about Cecil, Lord Hake, newly burst on local horizons. The one-column cut was of a young man with long, lean features, and a happy smile. His eyes were free from worry. He was a stranger to me, but one characteristic of his face reminded me of McCracken. And the pattern suddenly came clear. I knew why Flynne had been killed.

I took from my pocket the clipping I had found in the bag in Flynne's room and showed it to Melva. "Do you know what clipping service that's from?"

"I think it's Miller's," she hazarded. "If you'd get more publicity, I might become familiar with them."

"Get them on the phone for me, and leave the room."

"But they're in New York!"

"I am under the impression, pet, that even New York has telephones."

"I'll wind up in the poorhouse yet," she said. "Murders that threaten your career, and now long distance calls."

After considerable delay and telephone costs, I got the information I wanted. I rang Lord Hake next. He was in the hotel bar.

"Hake here," he said.

"This is George Sanders, Lord Cecil. It occurred to me that you and I probably have acquaintances in common. Such as Percy Wellesley."

"Yes, I know him."

"And others?" I suggested.

"Not a doubt, old boy."

"I'm giving a party for a few friends tonight. Will you come?"

"It will be a welcome change from society teas, Mr. Sanders. Eightish?"

Chapter Twenty-Six

FRED AND MELVA broke out of their samba routine as the record ended and came over to my built-in bar. Melva was in highnecked black, and her hair was a red-gold crown.

It was a dressy party. Everybody except Wallingford wore formal dress to some degree, with Riegleman topping the list in white tie and tails. They ran the gamut of fashion, from Listless, in backless blue, to the electricians, in white jackets and boiled shirts.

They sat and stood around in small groups. Now and then a voice raised above the others to fling a gem out of the mild hubbub.

"I thought her dress looked like an old fire hose."

". . . and his speech sounded like Tagalog in a high wind."

". . . it wasn't at Ciro's, it was the Troc."

Fred and Melva perched on stools, and his long face was solemn. "Don't call me Reverend, bartender. I wish to be as the others, common. Sister Bellows and I find that our best work is accomplished when we simulate wickedness."

"You have testimonials?" I asked.

243

"Indubitably."

He gave me a sheaf of papers. They were the reports on Carla, Riegleman, and Wanda. I began to read.

"Ahem," Melva said. "In our work, we cannot do our best with dry throats. A glass of ginger ale, please."

"Just scotch for me, bartender," Fred said. "My stomach is too weak for carbonated beverages."

I fixed their drinks, and ran through the reports. I found nothing significant.

"These are the last?" I asked Fred.

"Best I could do in this amount of time. Do you want more?"

"I don't think it will be necessary."

"Do you mean you know who it was?" Fred demanded.

"I think so. I'll clinch it tonight. Your telegram tipped me the identity of Lord Hake. How did you know?"

"I knew I'd seen him somewhere," Fred said. "I thought you'd translate that wire. Tell me who's the culprit, George, and I'll fix up a release. Do you keep a typewriter here in the rumpus room?"

"Wait, Fred. I'm not certain. I want to get a game started. If Lord Hake isn't here in a few minutes, I'll start without him."

"Poker or blackjack? Anyway, deal me in."

"This is a spelling game," I said.

"Aw, George! You sound like a high school picnic."

"I have a reason for it," I said. "I don't want any objections from you."

"You can't stop me from thinking."

"I've been trying to start you thinking," Melva said, "since I saw you kicked off that freight train."

They went away, bickering happily, and I waited for the doorbell to announce Lord Cecil. The boom-crew trio came over for a drink. Wanda drifted over in a sheath of green satin. She was a siren again.

Time passed. No Lord Hake. I rapped on the bar.

"Last call," I said, "before the festivities."

Nobody moved. They watched me idly.

"What I have in mind is this," I went on. "We make the stake a dime. I will give each of you in turn a group of three letters. Within fifteen seconds, you are to give me a word containing those three letters. If you take longer than that, you lose a dime, and vice versa. For example, if I give you c-q-x, you snap back at me with 'quixotic' or some other word with those letters. If you don't, you give me a dime."

"I will give you a dime now, George," Wallingford said. "I will even make you a loan, if you can't make the rent here."

"Charley can't spell," said the electrician named Joe. "Could he just make his mark?"

"No, listen," I said. "I'm serious. This is a good game. You'll like it."

"I got to have a lot more drinks before I like parlor games," Sammy declared. He came over, moving his bulk across the floor with an airy, surprising grace. "I better start now."

"But what does 'quixotic' *mean?*" Listless asked Wallingford.

"Didn't you ever eat Quaker Oats?" he replied.

"I'm perfectly willing to play," Curtis offered. "And after all, Mr. Sanders is our host."

"So what?" Joe demanded. "If he don't like this party, let him go somewhere else."

"I am afraid," I said grimly, "that I must insist on your taking part in this game."

"Don't you think it's a bit childish, George, old boy?"

I glared at Riegleman. He stood, cool, and suave, by the Capehart, and looked at me with amused condescension.

"I'm not childish!" I snapped. "I have a very sound reason for wishing to play this game."

"I'll play a game with you, George," Wanda said in a sultry voice. "But it won't be a spelling contest."

From the tail of my eye, I saw Wallingford look at her as if he'd never seen her before.

"If you don't pay any attention to him," Joe advised, "maybe it'll wear off."

"George," Wallingford said, "you have a nice cuppa coffee, black, and go to sleep for a while on this couch. I'll move."

"I haven't had even one drink—" I began.

Joe leaped to his feet. He swayed gently. "Then come fill the cup," he declaimed, "and in the fire of Spring your something of something something fling. What're we waiting for, Charley?"

They advanced upon me, and Listless said to Wallingford, "I know that one. Sammy used to recite it to me. 'The bird of time has but a little way to something, and the bird is on the wing'. What is that word, Sammy?"

"My God!" Wallingford said.

Joe and Charley came behind the bar.

"Take it easy, boys," I said. "I'm getting angry."

They grabbed me. I didn't struggle. I didn't want the place to become a shambles. They pulled and tugged, moving me from behind the bar. Their hauling took on a rhythm. As if on cue, they began to sing,

"Roll out the barrel, we'll have a barrel of fun."

The boom crew came over and joined in with some fancy harmony. Sammy grabbed Listless and began a snake dance. Soon, everybody was in it, whirling Indian-fashion around me in step to the "Beer Barrel Polka," which I loathe.

I had to smile. The situation was completely idiotic. My clenched hands relaxed. Charley and Joe piloted me to a low couch, eased me gently upon a pile of cushions, and Carla came to sit at my feet. Somebody put a drink in my hand, and they all went back to their conversations.

"This is a nice party," Carla said.

I had to grin, but my purpose took the grin away in a moment. "Let me try this thing on you, Carla. See if you don't think it's a good game."

Her dark eyes took on a look of resignation. "All right," she sighed.

"M-d-u," I said.

She frowned for perhaps three seconds before her face lighted. "Murder?"

I gave her a dime.

"Why are you looking at me like that?" she demanded. "Are you ill, George?"

"I may be," I said. "Excuse me."

I went to the bar and fixed myself a drink. Wanda came over. "George, I think Wally is seeing me in a new light. I catch a look now and then in his eyes. Oh, I hope it means I'm through with Mother Hubbards!"

"I hope so, too, Wanda," I said abstractedly. I focussed on her. "Let me try you on my game."

"Oh, George! I'm having so much fun."

"This won't take but a second," I said grimly. "N-e-n. Try that."

"Oh, all right," she growled. "Flynne. Or are proper names admissible?"

I gave her a dime. "Is everybody a mind-reader?" I muttered. I went back to the group. I didn't even excuse myself to Wanda.

Riegleman was standing apart, tall and distinguished, looking on. I was beginning to feel like a schoolboy asking a girl for his first date. "Enjoying yourself?" I asked.

"Very good party," he said pleasantly. "Those electricians are good fun."

"They're cards, all right."

"Their antics gave me an idea for a scene in my next picture. I'd like to discuss it with you, as soon as possible. Not here, of course. How about dinner tomorrow?"

"Why don't you come here? I'm a fair amateur chef."

"Delighted. At eight?"

"Righto. Listen, Riegleman, that game of mine

isn't really childish. Let me show you. All I do is give you—"

His blue eyes picked up ice cubes from somewhere, then the ice melted. He smiled fleetingly. "Lay on, MacDuff."

"M-d-c."

He frowned into his glass. He frowned at the ceiling. Seconds ticked away. I felt a small elation, a growing suspense. This hesitation began to assume the same significance as the pause in psychiatric association tests. He had the word close to his consciousness, but his subconscious would not allow him to say "homicide."

At eighteen seconds, he grinned suddenly, and said, "Homicide. I could think of nothing for a moment but midchannel, and I didn't think that would be allowed. How long?"

I told him, and he gave me a dime. "The game does have possibilities, George, old boy."

My face was beginning to get rather grim as I wandered over to a corner where Wallingford was trying to break away from a childhood tale by Listless. He saw me. "Just the man," he cried. "Excuse me, honey, I got to talk to George."

We walked away, and presently leaned against an electric horse. "Why do women got to remember when they were all legs and no teeth?" he demanded. "Pigtails yet! Better she should stick to hanging up dresses."

"She's a nice kid, Wally."

"Me, I like 'em with teeth. Even for telling about."

"Wally, let me try you on my game. I think you'll—"

"George, listen." He looked at his wrist watch. "I got to go. I got to give the baby his bath."

"At eleven o'clock?"

"It's easier when he's asleep. George, I liked your party, and—"

"Wally, this won't take fifteen seconds."

He sighed. "Grown men yet," he muttered.

"L-g-l," I said.

Instantly, he gave me a list. "Killing, rolling, calling, pulling, and gallon. Now give me a dime, George, and let it be a lesson. Better you should cut out dolls. It don't cost so much. Still," he added reflectively, "it depends on the doll."

I gave up. I went over to the bar and sat on a stool. Each person had come up with a word related to death or murder. Instead of avoiding it, they'd leaped at it. Sanders the brilliant, Sanders the wise, Sanders the great psychiatrist.

The doorbell reminded me that my most important guest had not arrived. This must be Lord Hake. I closed the rumpus room door behind me and answered the bell.

"Are you a magnet for crime?" Lamar James demanded. "Where's your telephone?"

"What do you mean, and what are you doing here?"

"Telephone!" he snapped.

I took him into the den, cut out the amplifying system on the phone, and he called for an ambulance. He hung up, looked at me.

"You've got a near corpse out there, George."

I followed him outside. Under a row of hydrangeas was an evening-clothed body. James put a flashlight on the figure of a young man whose fair hair was matted with blood.

He was Lord Hake.

Chapter Twenty-Seven

FINALLY, ALL WERE gone except Lieutenant Archer of the homicide squad, Lamar James, and myself. Archer put his notebook away.

"I guess that's it," he said. "Some thug knocked him out and robbed him."

"Then why the repeated blows?" James objected. "It looks like attempted murder."

Archer smiled tolerantly. "When you have seen as many evidences of crime as I have, you begin to accept the obvious. We don't try to put the worst possible construction on minor crime down here."

James flushed. He said nothing.

"Nobody saw anything, and all your guests arrived in groups of two or more," Archer said. "Nobody went outside after arrival. If Deputy Sheriff James hadn't dawdled on the doorstep after ringing the bell, even he would not have seen the guy. The ambulance doc said that the body must have lain there between four and five hours. That adds up to one thing: he was probably your first guest, and was slugged as he rounded that turn in your walk that hides a person from the street. If the poor lug recovers consciousness, he may be able to verify that. Well, so long, boys. I have all the names and addresses. If I want to ask any more questions, I know where to find everybody."

I let him out. James stared at me as I came back and mixed drinks. "Well?" he said presently.

"Well what?"

"What's your story this time?"

I frowned at him. "I don't like your tone, James."

"And I don't like your glib explanations, Sanders. Lord Hake was Herman Smith, wasn't he?"

"What makes you think so?" I stalled.

"The lower half of his face was lighter in color than the rest. He's shaved off a beard recently. Smith had a beard. Smith disappeared right after that accident in England. I figure he was the younger brother, a remittance man, who inherited when his older brother wrecked his Daimler."

"That was my conclusion. I verified his identity by telephoning a New York clipping service."

"You invited him here tonight?"

"Yes, but nobody else knew that."

"You knew it," he said.

"What do you mean by that?"

"When you gave me that yarn up north," James began steadily, as if he were addressing a complete stranger, "I told you it sounded phony. Missing guns, missing film. You didn't kill Paul—but I've got that figured out, too. Those inventions you've been talking about. You're perfectly capable of rigging up something that would kill him by remote control."

My jaw dropped. "In the dark? From a distance?"

"I'll admit it's a trifle far-fetched," he said, "but so is a criminal detector."

"I was joshing."

"That's what *you* say. I told you the camera wasn't on your hands when Peggy got it. You could have shot her."

"Don't be a fool!"

"I'm not being a fool. You're English. Hake is English. He comes into money. You show me a clipping you claim you got from Flynne's bag. How do I know you got it there?"

"Isn't it pretty obvious?" I asked hotly. "Smith loaned Flynne the bag. The clipping was in it."

"Your explanations are too smooth, Sanders. Here's the way it looks. You didn't know Smith by sight. So when some guy hands in his work slip, you assume it's Smith. So you plug him. Then you find out it's the wrong guy. You know Peggy saw you. You plug her. Paul figures it out, and tries to blackmail you. You plug him. But still you haven't got the guy you were after. So you talk the sheriff into letting you come back here. You invite Hake to the party, and ask him to come earlier than the others. You waylay him and ditch him where he won't be seen until the party breaks up. I think my job is finished now."

"I won't bother to argue," I said. "I have proof. I found that missing reel of film."

"You did, eh?" he drawled.

"I can prove that too," I snapped. "Because I'm going to run it for you right now." The surprise on his face pleased me. "Almost the first thing I did when I got back from location was develop and print it. So just sit back and watch."

"Wait a minute. You have to turn the lights out?"

"Naturally."

"Then I'll handcuff you. If you're innocent, you won't mind."

"I don't mind at all," I snarled. "May I set up the projector first?"

"Sure. I can watch you. Don't make any funny moves."

I forced myself to cool off as I threaded film. The circumstances did warrant his loose conclusions.

He handcuffed me. I flicked off the lights, started the projector. He watched in silence.

The wagon train came across the dunes at sunrise. I cut a handsome figure on the creamy Arabian, and the close-ups made it obvious that Carla and I had what polite people would refer to as an Understanding.

Now came the critical scene. I was in the foreground, naturally, but we could see Severance Flynne, out of focus, in the background. I galloped up and down, shouting, pointing and then firing the silver-mounted pistols. At a moment when I was facing the camera, looking lustfully at an off-stage Carla, Severance Flynne was shot.

He straightened from his crouch in one convulsive movement and seemed to leap several feet to one side where he fell, kicked a few times, and lay still. The action was so realistic that it detracted from my close-up.

When it was done, I turned the lights on. James grinned ruefully.

"That certainly lets you out," he said. "I apologize."

I held out my wrists. He removed the cuffs. I was still miffed. "I ought to knock you across the room."

"Sure, but let's finish that drink. So what's the story? You know more than you've told."

"In the first place, I didn't ask Lord Hake to come early. He suggested eight o'clock. I asked the others to come at nine, which they did. I wanted to verify a few ideas of mine, and Hake could give me confirmation."

"Such as?"

"I have no proof," I objected. "I'm going to make a phone call later. If Hake comes to, he can tell me. Otherwise, I'll have to try something else."

James got to his feet. "Well, let me know."

"Come out to the set in the morning," I said. "Maybe I'll have something then."

"You'd better. You've only got two days to deliver on that sappy promise to those reporters."

After he had gone, I began to agree with his description of my promise. I put in a call to London.

The first person I saw on the set the next morning was the beard. I nodded to him. "Still sore?"

"In spirit, no," he said. "I carry my own cushion, however, to sit on. I want to tell you, Mr. Sanders, how I appreciate the job you're doing on *Seven Dreams.*"

I blinked. Why should he care? "Thanks," I said shortly.

Riegleman came into the big sound stage, and after him the technicians. "Blast the blasted writing profession," Riegleman said. "I suppose we'll do those mission shots today. If I ever catch up with that Connaught person, I'll make him wish he'd never sharpened a pencil."

The beard interrupted. "Mr. Riegleman—"

Riegleman gave him the icy eye. "You're not needed today! Only the principals are in this scene. Who in the bloody hell let you in here, anyway?"

"Mr. Wallingford brought me in."

"What the hell for?" Riegleman demanded.

"I went over to see Mr. Wallingford last night, and I told him—"

"I see," Riegleman said curtly. "And you talked him into giving you a bit part. Well, I've got no place for you. You'll have to wait until that brainless author shows up, and I don't care if B. G. Wexel himself says you should have a close-up. I'll let you know when you're wanted."

He turned back to me, but the beard tugged his sleeve. "Mr. Riegleman, Mr. Wallingford expressly told me—"

Riegleman whirled, white with fury. "I told you—" He paused and looked at the beard, slit-eyed. "What are you doing here, and who are you?"

"I'm Arthur Connaught," the beard said.

There was one of those silences that simply can't be described.

Riegleman stood perfectly still. His face looked as though it had gotten stuck. At last he said, "You're— who?"

"Arthur Connaught," the beard repeated. He looked surprised, as though we should have known it all the time.

I grabbed the back of a chair and held on to it tight. Riegleman sank down in one and stared.

"You're Arthur Connaught, the author," he breathed. "Then why in the hell did you play in the mob scene, bobbling on a horse as if it were a typhoon?"

"I'm sorry about the horse," Connaught said apologetically. "You see, I'd never been on one before. I hope I didn't ruin any film."

"That reel was lost, fortunately," Riegleman said. The color began to come back to his face. "Didn't you know we were looking high and low for you—?"

Connaught—I still thought of him as The Beard— shook his head and looked unhappy. "My agent told me to report on location. When I got there, someone shoved me into a line. There was a sign saying 'Beards this way.' I don't know much about the motion picture business, Mr. Riegleman. So I just did as I was told."

Riegleman and I looked at each other. Then we both looked at Arthur Connaught. While everybody had been searching for him, he'd been playing an extra, a beard, in the story he'd written. Getting a thousand dollars a week for it, too. I wondered how the business office would ever straighten that out on the budget.

"Never mind," Riegleman said at last, and very gently. "Anything can happen in this business."

"Authors should never wear beards," I added consolingly. "They're confusing. Besides, they draggle in the ink."

Connaught's eyes met mine for an instant. For the first time I saw a smile fleet across his face.

Then Riegleman sighed and said, "Well, we're making a picture. Or trying to make one. We've got to have a scene—"

"I stayed up all night at Mr. Wallingford's," Connaught said, "and wrote the scene. He explained what he wanted."

Riegleman was annoyed. "Let me have a look at it."

"Mr. Wallingford is getting the mimeographed copies."

We stood waiting. Connaught wandered about, happy as an ant in a cupboard. He regarded the generators, cables, lights, and cameras, with a look of childish wonder.

Wallingford came in presently with a stack of paper in one arm and Carla on the other. "Quiet!" Wallingford cried. "We got to work fast, losing all that time up north." He dealt out copies of the script to me, to Connaught, to Carla, Riegleman, Sammy, and the new script girl. "All night I stayed up to get this finished. Maybe you can give me a little of your time today. Page 85 A it starts. Not much dialogue. I don't like words, so maybe we can shoot it after one rehearsal. Somebody bring in that cave."

Prop men brought in the cave. Artists put a desert backdrop behind it. Electricians yelled for lights while Curtis directed stand-ins and made measurements. Sammy darted about, flinging orders here and there. Riegleman wandered off to a dark corner. Connaught grinned delightedly at this storm before the calm.

I retired to a quiet place to run through the scene, and Lamar James came up to say hello. I nodded absently, and he joined Connaught.

The scene was easily learned. It opened in this shelter from a sudden storm. Carla and I had appropriated it for our own. We had no more than half a dozen lines each, before a hail from the storm was to herald her husband descending upon us.

"I'm ready to go through it," I called to Carla. She nodded her readiness, and we walked toward the cave.

"I want a drink of water, George. Shall I bring you one?"

"Please."

She went off into the gloom behind the lights, and I sat down to wait for her and Riegleman, who was still absent. Carla was back in a moment, and Riegleman was not far behind. He was watching her with a peculiar expression which seemed to be composed of worry and bewilderment. She gave me the water, and I raised the paper cup to my lips.

A strong, bitter odor assailed my nostrils. I sniffed again and looked at Carla.

"What's the matter?" she cried. "Don't look at me like that! What's the matter, George?"

Quiet fell, broken by Lamar James as he pounded over to me. He took the cup, sniffed, and spoke steadily to Carla.

"It is my duty to warn you that anything you may say may be used against you. You are under arrest for attempted murder."

Carla fainted. One of the prop men caught her. James told them to carry her outside. He turned to Wallingford. "You have chemists here. I want to have this analyzed. I won't take her away until I'm sure."

Wallingford seemed broken. "Poor Carla," he said. His round face had sagged. He seemed ancient. "She must have had an awful good reason. Come on, Mr. James. I show you myself the laboratory."

I looked at Riegleman. He was staring after James and Wallingford. I went over to him. He gave me a kind of sleepwalker's stare. "I'm—God, I'm stunned, George! I—" He dropped his arms loosely in despair. "There isn't anything to say, I suppose."

"I can say thanks," I said. "If it hadn't been for the expression on your face, I'd have tossed off that water straightaway."

He looked at me thoughtfully. "I—see," he said. Then he shrugged and called out, "That's all for today. We'll let you know when and if work on the picture is to be resumed." He turned back to me. "It will be difficult to replace Carla. Perhaps we had better discuss the picture at dinner tonight, and make plans to go ahead with it."

"All right." We looked steadily at each other for a tense moment.

I went off to look for Lamar James. The analysis was finished when I found him in the laboratory.

"It's cyanide," he said. "Enough to kill a horse or two."

"I want to tell you about my telephone," I said.

Chapter Twenty-Eight

RIEGLEMAN ARRIVED at seven o'clock instead of eight.

"I was curious to know what we were eating tonight," he explained as I took his coat.

"Steak and kidney pie," I said.

He gave me a look compounded of speculation and knowledge. "Rather significant, what?" he said.

"Come out to the kitchen and I'll give you a glass of sherry. I'm about to make the pastry before I light the oven."

He followed me, and sat down in the breakfast nook, facing me. "Significant?" I repeated. "I don't know. Your use of the idiom didn't penetrate for some time because I was accustomed to that usage. I should have pegged you for an Englishman long ago."

From the icebox I took the flour, shortening, and water. I chilled a silver knife and began to cut the shortening into the flour.

Riegleman sipped at his sherry. "This is good, George. Very dry. Yes, I thought you'd reached a conclusion, finally. I say, old boy, don't you use your hands on pastry?"

"Not unless necessary. It's lighter this way."

"My mother," he said, "always used her hands. She never measured anything. She took a handful of this, a pinch of that, and her pastry was wonderful."

"Cooking by touch," I said. "There are a few geniuses who do that. I get my best results by following the rules." I mixed the flour and shortening with the chilled knife, and added ice water a dollop at a time.

"I hope, for your sake, that the meal is good, George."

"It will be. I'm using a T-bone instead of round steak. And, if I were you, I shouldn't worry about me."

"Ah?" he murmured. "Very well. What is that contraption?" He pointed to the electric dicer.

"I made it," I told him. "It cuts steak, or anything else, into small cubes." I began to roll the dough on my aluminum board, sifting flour over it now and then.

"You're an ingenious fellow, George. It's too bad."

"Oh, I don't know," I said lightly. "I like it this way."

"That's what I mean, old boy. It's too bad you like it."

"There," I said. "We'll have a light, thick crust. I think it will be flaky. Now for the steak. You see, I start the dicer and feed the steak to it a bit at a time. See how clean and uniform the cuts are?"

"Very nice," he said. "What kind of kidney have you?"

"Lamb, of course. Just wait until I chop this onion

and get this mess into a frying pan. Do you like a great deal of butter?"

"Use a lavish hand," Riegleman said. "We should enjoy this meal."

"Will you have more sherry?"

"Please. Thank you."

I gave him the bottle, and poured myself a taste. It had a nice nutty flavor. "That *is* good sherry. Shall we drink a toast to tomorrow?"

"Whatever it brings, George?"

"Whatever."

We touched glasses, drank. I began to sauté the steak, and parboil the lamb kidney. When I had this going, I began to sauté the mushrooms. Riegleman watched me, his long face full of regret.

"Do you make your own salad dressing?" he asked.

"Yes. I chiseled the receipe from my favorite French restaurant. It's difficult to get fresh thyme, though."

"You know, George, you have a nerve."

I shrugged. "I'm confident, that's all."

"But you have every reason not to be."

"Not from my viewpoint."

"You'll admit I had rotten luck."

"I'll do nothing of the sort," I said. "It was carelessness, nothing more."

"But I hadn't seen the boy since he was sixteen, and beards *are* confusing, you know."

"You're his cousin. I telephoned Percy Wellesley in London. He said you were."

"Yes. Say, that smells good!"

"It bakes now for thirty minutes. Shall we go into the living room? Have more sherry."

"Thanks." He motioned me to precede him, waved me to my big chair. He sat, facing me, on a divan. His eyes were bright and sparkling now.

"You were too observant," he said conversationally.

"I wasn't observant enough," I corrected him. "It should have been obvious that you had Peggy's notebook, and had studied it, when you made me change my tie."

"I made a bad mistake there," he admitted. One corner of his mouth curled into what, under other circumstances, might have been a smile. "A reel of film was missing, but I had a feeling it would be found. If you'd worn the wrong tie, an expensive scene would have had to be retaken. Having studied the notebook the night before, I suddenly forgot my real role and for a moment or so I was just a director who had to watch the budget."

"I never knew you to have an eye for details before," I said. "Peggy always tended to them. That was my bad mistake, not getting the full implication of that tie business at once."

He said, "Really, George, you did well, considering that you had nothing to work with but falsities."

"The truth was there before my eyes."

"And you saw it eventually, old man. You knew the first shot came from behind the camera. You finally decided that nobody else could have fired it."

"No, it wasn't that simple. I considered everybody, even the girl in wardrobe."

"Surely it had to be me!"

"I see that now," I said. "But I didn't for some

time. What threw me off was your indifference to Flynne's death."

"Why should I have cared?" he asked reasonably. "I shot the wrong person. I had no motive. Therefore, I shouldn't be suspected, provided I forgot all about it."

"But Peggy figured it out."

"She was my greatest danger," he admitted. "Her notebook was too damned omniscient."

"I put it together this way," I said. "She questioned a piece of business at the moment Flynne was shot, and started to ask you. You were gone, and she made a note of it. The next day, she remembered you were gone and suddenly wondered."

"It was something like that, George. Flynne's death throes were too dramatic. An extra was stealing the scene. She thought it should be retaken. Of course," he said, "I was too hasty. Peggy didn't really know anything, and she'd have dismissed the thought. But I was nervous. When I saw her put her hand to her mouth—" He paused. "Still, perhaps it was best. I couldn't chance her raising the point of my temporary absence."

"You were behind the sound truck."

."Yes."

"What did you do with the guns?"

"I have one of them with me, of course."

"The bullet will be identified. You'll be caught."

He nodded. "Yes. This is a matter of personal revenge, now. Young Hake recovered about an hour ago. He'll tell that deputy all the facts. You are responsible for my blunder in killing Peggy, and I'm going to even my score with you."

"How am I responsible?"

"Your reputation, old boy. You are *The Falcon* and *The Saint*. After I discovered that Flynne was the wrong man, I thought: Sanders will smell out the lack of motive, find that I thought the man was Herman Smith, and identify Smith. I shouldn't have killed Peggy, otherwise."

"It was your artistic integrity, rather than that logical sequence of deducting, that made me certain," I said. "Yesterday, you accused Connaught of bobbing on his horse as though the beast was a typhoon. Peggy must have noted that in her book. You wouldn't have paid any attention to him otherwise. You never noticed such details. You always left them to someone else."

"By that time I was certain that you were on to me, George. That, of course, is why I put the cyanide in the water I drew for Carla to give you. Too bad you didn't take it."

"I belong to the opposite school of thought," I said. "I'm glad I didn't. By the way, I owe you a lump on the head. You shouldn't have hit me."

"Sheer panic," he said. "I regretted it instantly."

"Thanks. There's one thing I don't understand, Riegleman. Why did you use a thirty-eight? All the guns were forty-fives."

"Not yours, George. You carried thirty-eights. I figured that the gun would be found on you, and the whole affair passed off as an accident."

"Why did you plant the gun in Carla's wagon, then?"

"That was no plant. I simply put it there to remove

later. When you brought up the question of murder, I had to leave it and hope for the best."

"And you killed the wrong man."

"Amusing, isn't it?"

"Not to him."

"I daresay," Riegleman said thoughtfully, "that he is better off. There are too many extras."

"That dish is cooked by now," I said. "Shall we have dinner?"

He got to his feet. "I think not. You doubtless planned for that deputy to arrive at eight and eavesdrop on our conversation. And to arrest me when I'd made a damaging statement. That's why I arrived an hour early, not that it matters now."

"I expected you to arrive an hour early," I said, with an attempt at casualness.

"A bad attempt at a bluff, George. Naturally, I didn't underestimate you. I watched the house for two hours before I came in, to make certain you didn't set any traps."

He sniffed at the tantalizing odor from the kitchen. "Too bad about the meal, old boy, but I think we had better toddle along."

I got to my feet, too, and moved so that when he faced me his back was toward the open bedroom door. "I'm not going with you, Riegleman."

"Oh, I think so," he said pleasantly. "You don't wish to be killed here, do you?"

"Not here or anywhere. In fact, I'm not going to be killed."

"Oh, I think so." He was still pleasant. "I've rather

developed a taste for killing. It makes one somewhat like God. Power of life and death, and all that."

"That isn't why you killed Paul. It was because he asked you about Herman Smith. He remembered that Smith was a remittance man, and would inherit if his father and elder brother died."

Riegleman nodded. "I overheard Paul telephone a friend here in Hollywood and corroborate that fact. When he headed toward your trailer, I killed him. I still hoped, at that time, to get away with it."

"I see. I was wrong on a few details, but I came out at the right door."

"You did very well. Shall we go now?"

"Wait a moment. How did you know Lord Cecil was coming to my party?"

"I invited him, of course."

"Why, so did I."

Riegleman smiled. "So I learned. I pretended to be you on the telephone, and it was confusing for a while. I explained that I had—or you had—invited so many that it had slipped your mind. So he said he wanted to talk to you, and would come early. He was going to identify me as his cousin, who was the next of kin. The title wouldn't pass to me, but the money would."

"The money has always been your first consideration," I said. "You waylaid him, tried to kill him, left him for dead, and waited for somebody to arrive?"

"I drove down the street and parked until Wally arrived in a cab. I came in with him, you remember?"

"I hadn't noticed. Did you use a hammer on Lord Cecil?"

"Yes, it's in my toolbox. I haven't decided yet whether to use it or a gun on you. Which would you prefer?"

"Hammers are messy," I said. "You wouldn't want to go down in criminal history as a hammer slayer, would you?" I spoke casually, but I could feel every drop of ice-cold sweat on my forehead. "Besides, you're not going to kill me. I knew you meant to, when I saw your expression yesterday on the set. But naturally, I'm against it."

His eyes took on a slight glaze. He brought the gun out of his pocket. "I've got to kill you. Right here and now, if necessary."

"You won't," I said, "because Lamar James has you covered."

Riegleman grinned. An unpleasant grin. "That's a very old gag, George. You thought I was going to turn my head for a moment, and you'd have a chance to dive at me. Sorry. I know the gag too well. I've used it in some old B pictures myself."

Lamar James's voice said, right behind him, "Don't move, Riegleman. I won't kill you, because I want you to stand trial. But I'll shoot you at the base of the spine. That would hurt."

I'd always thought, "His face turned gray,". was a literary affectation. Watching Riegleman, I found out it could really happen. The gun sagged a little in his hand. He started to turn his head.

"Don't move," Lamar James said. "Hand your gun to George."

Riegleman did so. I gripped it. It felt comfortably reassuring in my hand.

CRIME ON MY HANDS

"All right," I said, loudly. "You can come and get him now."

"Okay," Lamar James's voice said.

From the loudspeaker came the click of a telephone being cradled, and then the dial tone. Riegleman jerked his head toward it, then glared furiously at me.

"He was listening in his hotel room," I said. "He'll be along in a moment. I was afraid you might have remembered my telephone set-up here, but it probably wouldn't have mattered. I could have handled you anyway."

At least, I thought, *The Falcon,* and *The Saint* always could handle such situations. "I had to use the telephone set-up," I said, "because I didn't dare have anyone come here. I was afraid you'd be watching."

He started to move, and I raked his face with the gun barrel. He raised his hand to the cut.

"That's for Peggy," I said. "You shot her in the back. Just dare to move again, will you?"

Chapter Twenty-Nine

I T WAS LIKE an old-fashioned family reunion. Melva
looked ecstatic, and Fred was trying to talk into
four telephones at once. Wallingford came in just as
Carla was released from her cell and rushed into the
waiting room. While she mumbled a routine of in-
coherent thanks, Wallingford shook hands with
Lamar James, heaven knows why.

Wanda had come in with Wallingford, and she and
Carla dived at me simultaneously. Both of them began to trickle tears down my neck, while Wallingford
shook hands with the jailer, with Fred, and with a
man who'd come in to empty the wastebaskets. Everything sort of went all to pieces for a minute.

"Isn't it wonderful!" Wanda cried. "Wally's going
to let me do comedy. I'll be leading woman in your
next, George."

"George," Carla said, "I knew, I just knew you
wouldn't let me rot here. Oh, I thank you, I thank
you!"

"And I can wear a bathing suit in one scene,"
Wanda said.

Carla drew back. She looked coolly at Wanda. "How nice," she said. "Aren't you afraid?"

"Not at all, darling," Wanda said frostily. "Nor would you be—if you were I."

Carla shrugged. She turned to me. "What shall we do to celebrate, George?"

My pulse beat a trifle faster. She *was* very beautiful.

"You girls run along," Wallingford said crisply. "I lost a director just now. We got a picture to finish. Already, it's a big investment. George, maybe you can help out, huh?"

I just couldn't keep the delight out of my eyes. Not only was I playing Hilary Weston, I could direct the rest of the picture.

"Not for the money you're paying him," Melva began indignantly.

Wallingford waved a hand at her. "Tomorrow we talk business," he said expansively. "Meantime, have a cigar." He looked at Melva, caught himself, and said, "All right, have a cigarette. Take the whole pack. Women shouldn't be agents. A nice girl like you, too!"

I was in a kind of happy haze. I blinked, and realized that Wanda and Carla were looking at me. Not very amiably, either. Then they looked at each other.

"All right," Carla said. "We'll go celebrate without him."

"Fine," Wanda said. "After all, he's more interested in the picture than in us."

They went off arm in arm. I opened my mouth to call them back. Before I could speak, they said, almost in unison, "See you tomorrow, George."

I felt very lonely, all of a sudden.

Wallingford spoke to me three times before I became aware of him. "How is it, George? Do you direct, or not?"

"Sure, Wally. I'll be glad to."

"You don't sound glad."

"Listen," I said. "I've got a dinner at home, crying to be eaten. And I have to get there and take my phone apart to hang it up." I frowned. "There must be some way to fix it so it will hang up." I finished, "Why don't you two come home and have dinner with me?"

"If you feel the way you look," Lamar James said, "the food is spoiled."

"Stop worrying about the girls," Wallingford commanded. "They'll be back. And if they don't come back, some others will. If you stand long enough in one place, a good looker will be along."

"In the corridor of a jail?" I asked.

Wallingford stared wildly around at the row of cell doors. "Ever since this picture started, I been spending a lot of time in some jail! If it gets to be a habit, you're fired, George."

He grabbed my arm and hustled me out on the street. We got into Lamar James's car, and pulled out into traffic. Wallingford turned to me, and he seemed embarrassed.

"George, I got bad news."

"You mean I can't direct the picture after all?"

He grinned. "So you forgot about them girls already. No, this ain't about the picture, George. It's about that present I promised you. I can't get one. There ain't any."

I blinked, then remembered I had asked him for a transit, a 22-inch achromatic.

"It was a gag, Wally. There's one on Mount Wilson, I know, but it's very special. Maybe I can get an engineering outfit to make one just like it."

"Engineering?" he asked incredulously. "You crazy?"

"Why, no. I should think a manufacturer of engineering supplies should be able to build a transit."

"What's all this transit stuff?" he demanded.

"An achromatic, twenty-two inch transit. That's what I asked for."

"Oh!" he cried loudly. "And I wired every circus in the world for a twenty-two inch acrobat!"

THE LIBRARY OF CRIME CLASSICS

LESLIE CHARTERIS
Angels Of Doom
The First Saint Omnibus
Knight Templar
The Last Hero
The Saint in New York

CARROLL JOHN DALY
Murder from the East

LILLIAN DE LA TORRE
Dr. Sam: Johnson, Detector
The Detections of Dr. Sam:
Johnson
The Return of Dr. Sam:
Johnson, Detector
The Exploits of Dr. Sam:
Johnson, Detector

PETER DICKINSON
Perfect Gallows

PAUL GALLICO
The Abandoned
Love of Seven Dolls
Mrs.'Arris Goes To Paris
Farewell To Sport
Too Many Ghosts
Thomasina

JAMES GOLLIN
Eliza's Galliardo
The Philomel Foundation

DOUGLAS GREENE &
ROBERT ADEY
Death Locked In
DASHIELL HAMMETT &
ALEX RAYMOND
Secret Agent X-9

REGINALD HILL
A Killing Kindness

RICHARD HULL
The Murder of My Aunt

E. RICHARD JOHNSON
Cage 5 Is Going To Break
Dead Flowers
The God Keepers
The Inside Man
Mongo's Back in Town
Silver Street

JONATHAN LATIMER
Headed for a Hearse
The Lady in the Morgue
Murder In the Madhouse
The Search for My Great
Uncle's Head
Solomon's Vineyard

VICTORIA LINCOLN
A Private Disgrace
Lizzie Borden by Daylight

MARGARET MILLAR
An Air That Kills
Ask for Me Tomorrow
Banshee
Beast in View
Beyond This Point Are
Monsters
The Cannibal Heart
The Fiend
Fire Will Freeze
How Like An Angel
The Iron Gates
The Listening Walls
The Murder of Miranda
Rose's Last Summer
Spider Webs
A Stranger in My Grave
Vanish In An Instant
Wall of Eyes

Write For Our Free Catalog:
International Polygonics, Ltd.
Madison Square, P.O. Box 1563
New York, NY 10159